MEMOIRS OF A SWINGER COUPLE
-Sex and Friendship

MEMOIRS OF A SWINGER COUPLE
-Sex and Friendship

Joakim & Susanne Andersson

Prologue

This is my and my wife's story of our first ten years in the swinger world. Great emphasis has been placed on not revealing either our own or anyone else's identity. All personal names are fictitious, the locations of the clubs correspond to reality but other locations are mostly fictitious. In all other respects, the book's events correspond to reality as far as our memories go. Dialogues and detailed descriptions of intimate events are, of course, difficult to reproduce exactly, but have been recreated with the help of feelings and shared memories.

The story was first published in Swedish in 2015, but since swinging is an international phenomenon, we now want to share our story on a larger scale. If anyone is wondering if we are still part of the swinger world ten years later, the answer is yes, but with some difference. When we meet our swinger friends, we often put more emphasis on socializing than sex, but on the other hand, one doesn't necessarily exclude the other…

Personally, I would also like to express my gratitude to my dear wife and co-author. Despite, or rather thanks to, the path we chose, she is a faithful life partner and has been an excellent sounding board and mainstay in the writing process. Her wise retorts and often demanding suggestions for changes in the text have been of great help in developing the plot. Above all, I appreciate her for wholeheartedly supporting and believing in the book project throughout the process.

Joakim and Susanne, Stockholm, Sweden November 2024

All journeys start somewhere, ours began on a ferry between Finland and Sweden

Susanne, I'm going to a fair in Turku in two weeks. Bosse had to cancel the trip due to some medical problem with his mother. There's no point in flying so I'll take the ferry."

"Then you will be alone?"

"Maybe not, can't you take a few days off? I'm leaving early on Thursday and I'll be back on Friday night. If you come along, we'll have Thursday night to ourselves in Turku and I have a cabin booked until home, I will actually be at the fair most of Friday, but then you can spend the day sightseeing and shopping."

"That sounds nice, but I'll have to check with Erik if that's okay. We have a few busy weeks ahead of us as we start renovating the reception. It will mean a little extra work for me, but a few days off shouldn't be impossible."

"I think the old slave driver has a good eye for you, doesn't he?"

"Sure, he likes me but I still need to talk to him. Anyway, he's not as grumpy and boring as you might think if you don't know him. When do you need my answer?"

"Don't worry, everything is booked, but hmm ... if you come with me, we could upgrade to a better cabin. It will be great, make sure you get time off so we can have some fun in the disco on the way back."

And of course, Susanne's vacation worked out ... After a packed day in Turku, she meets up with Joakim at the hotel for the return trip.

"Joakim, I had a great day! I saw some of old Turku, but mostly I ran around in shops. You would have gotten tired of me."

"Nah, do you really think so?" Joakim replies with feigned surprise.

I think so, or rather, I know ... I probably spent a couple of hours in the stores at Hansa Shopping Centre. It's only five minutes from the hotel. Not exactly same stores as at home, actually did some real bargains," says Susanne, spinning around in a pirouette. "Including these shoes, aren't they fabulous!"

"Super cool, absolutely my style. Did you have lunch at the shopping center or at the hotel?"

"Neither, I found a cozy little café in the market hall where I had a chicken salad and a glass of wine. After that, I strolled around among all the stalls. It was so nice just walking around and experiencing all the lovely scents. You would have loved it. Not to mention the market hall itself, it's beautiful. The tourist map I got at the hotel said it was built in the late nineteenth century, it must be one of Turku's most beautiful buildings."

"It sounds like you had a really good day," Joakim says.

"Absolutely. But what about you, how was the fair?"

"Pretty good, there were two ... maybe three interesting exhibitors. Especially a Finnish company that I hadn't heard of, their Swedish representative will contact me next week. Otherwise, there were no major news, mostly the same companies that exhibit in Sweden."

"Okay, so maybe that Finnish company is worth pursuing?"

"Maybe, I'll find out more about them next week."

"In any case, I'm glad I came along. It's just a shame we didn't choose an evening departure from Stockholm."

"You are absolutely right, eleven hours without a cabin is far too long.

"But it gets better on the way home, now we can party and go to bed when we feel like it."

"It's going to be great, an excellent end to a nice day. At first, I was actually a bit afraid that it would be boring to be alone all day, but it was actually nice not to have to consider anyone else. But clearly, I've missed you, and it's only gotten worse", says Susanne with a mischievous smile.

"What's gotten worse?"

"The tingle in the pussy, I really need a good fuck tonight."

"Oh, nothing else, I can absolutely help you with that," replies Joakim with a broad grin.

"Yes, some good food and dancing will probably be a good foreplay. When was the last time we went out dancing? It feels like an eternity, we should have time for this kind of thing more often."

"Absolutely, but now the taxi is here."

The taxi driver sighs and groans as he loads the shopping bags and suitcases. He doesn't exactly get happier when he realizes that it's only a short drive to the ferry terminal. With a bang, he slams the trunk shut and sinks into the driver's seat, continuing to sigh and grumble. Behind the wheel, however, he seems to get a new energy. They are barely in place before he dives into the busy Friday traffic in Turku. In an attempt to initiate a conversation with the grumpy driver, Susanne asks a question about the castle, but the answer is meager, just a short answer in Finnish. As a sign that the conversation is over for him, he demonstratively turns up the volume on the radio. The radio host utters some incomprehensible words that end with a name they recognize, and soon Meredith Brooks' suggestive voice fills the car. *Bitch,* her only but significant hit is apparently something that pleases the sour-faced driver. He unabashedly hums along and immediately looks much happier.

"Nice song," Joakim comments, and both he and Susanne try to keep up with the lyrics, which have a refreshing, erotic undertone.

"Good lyric, I believe I'm a little mixture of all that, but tonight I want to be more bitch than mother," Susanne says with a mischievous expression.

"Sure, I like it when you're bitchy."

"Oh yeah, but you better watch out!" Susanne says with a meaningful wink. "Tonight, I want to have real fun, I really hope the disco is okay."

"Full speed on the dance floor and then a sweaty ending in the cabin, does that suit madam?"

"Absolutely, sounds like an evening to my liking."

Once on board and after the usual search for their cabin, they are not disappointed.

"What a fantastic cabin," Susanne exclaims and gives Joakim a long-wet kiss. "We could even have a little party here."

"That would work just fine, but we'll have to entertain ourselves," Joakim says in a tone that cannot be misinterpreted.

As soon as they installed themselves in the cabin, and unpacking their evening clothes, they head out onto the deck. The autumn sun shines pale and weak as they glide past the last islands of Turku's enchanting beautiful archipelago. The sea air is icy cold; it already feels like winter even though it's only the beginning of October. Even the seagulls, who usually faithfully follow the ferries, have tucked themselves down in the cold wind. Their stay on the deck is not long-lasting; after just a few minutes, they decide that the restaurant is a much nicer place.

On arrival at the bustling restaurant, they regain their warmth while waiting to place their order. Disappointed, they note that the menu doesn't contain anything that truly excites their taste buds. They agree on a safe choice, salmon and a Chardonnay from Chile, which should be okay, at least considering the price. Surprisingly quickly, they get to place their order, but the Finnish ferries are no exception – you feel forgotten once you've placed your order. As usual, the wine arrives promptly, but the food takes time. Why is it always like that? The long-awaited food eventually arrives and tastes better than they expected; the chef clearly knows how to prepare salmon. They conclude the meal with coffee and liqueur and then head towards the disco. On the way, Susanne stops by the restroom and comes out with a happy expression.

"Joakim, I took off my panties; I felt too proper ..."

"Why am I not surprised?" Joakim responds with a smile.

At that moment, they hear a cheerful voice behind them, "I DIDN'T HEAR ANYTHING!"

They turn around and see a man with his hands over his ears, smiling widely. They smile back and continue towards the disco.

"That was actually quite funny; now he has something amusing to tell his friends," Susanne chuckles.

They find the disco on the next floor, and it is already overcrowded, but determinedly, they squeeze their way into the middle of the dance floor. The music is okay, and they soon enthusiastically join in the chaos at the dance floor; the evening looks promising.

The dance floor, filled with happy, smiling people, creates a seductive mix of sounds and scents. Joakim can't shake off the thoughts of Susanne's intimate area, where the panties, according to her own statement are absent. The atmosphere becomes more and more charged, their thoughts inevitably turn to sex. The embraces become longer and more intense with each new break. Joakim soon discovers that he can slip a hand under Susanne's dress without anyone noticing. In the next moment, he realizes that neither he nor Susanne care if anyone notices what they're up to.

Joakim whispers between two songs "I have to fuck you properly tonight."

"You can't get away even if you try," Susanne replies, while pressing her lower part of her body closer against him.

The playful touch continues, and Susanne also discovers that she can get close to Joakim. However, she quickly realizes that it is not easy to dance with one hand in Joakim's crotch. She withdraws her hand with an apologetic "I'll be back", in a valiant attempt to overpower the music.

The crowded dance floor further enhances the erotic atmosphere, making it impossible to avoid physical contact with other couples, but no one seems to mind either.

Susanne thinks about her panties in her purse, just the thought that she is hardly alone in freeing herself from this overrated garment increases the itch in her crotch.

A few dances later, Joakim yearns for something refreshing. They make their way to the bar and after some waiting, they finally get their drinks. The break and the drink, at least for the moment, give new life to their feet and bodies. But the most tangible feeling is still that tickling sensation in the lower part of their bodies waking up with renewed energy.

As soon as they finish the drinks, Susanne abruptly gets up and pulls Joakim up. "I'm so damn horny, let's go to the cabin!

Halfway there, they stop for a kiss, and Joakim immediately lets his hand slide under her dress.

"Do you feel how damn wet I am?" Susanne hisses.

Joakim can't do anything but agree and whispers back, "You're not just wet, your wonderful scent can be sensed from afar, you literally stink of cunt."

After a few more seconds, they passionately act like hormone-driven teenagers. Despite their state, they notice the older couple staring at them with wide eyes. Just the knowledge of having spectators makes them even more aroused, if possible. However, Susanne realizes they can't continue; it would be too much of a live show in a public place. She smoothly slips out of Joakim's embrace, and they continue to the privacy of the cabin. The dress, which, besides shoes and socks, is Susanne's only garment, quickly comes off. Joakim also hastily removes his clothes, clearly showing that he is ready. The erotic atmosphere that has been building up during the afternoon and evening reaches its peak.

After the few seconds it took to get undressed, Joakim pauses for a brief moment. He gazes at Susanne with eyes sparkling with both love and lust, but at this moment, the latter undoubtedly has the upper hand.

"Damn, you're delicious," he says while purposefully seeking out Susanne's moist, pulsating slit.

Susanne eagerly anticipates the touch she has been waiting for all evening, but Joakim makes her wait a little longer. He can't continue without inhaling her arousing scent, the same scent that has driven men to madness for millennia. He is well aware that this divine scent only lasts for a short while. It will soon be washed away by the orgasms impatiently waiting to take over Susanne's body and consciousness. From Susanne's perspective, Joakim's pleasurable yet prolonged treatment is moving her too slowly towards the enticing abyss of orgasm. She teeters on the edge, but Joakim doesn't let her get close enough to fall over it. Her body literally screaming for the ecstasy to be unleashed. She begs, demands that Joakim penetrate her. For Susanne, time seems to have stopped but ... finally, Joakim fulfills her hot desire. It only takes a few seconds before the familiar spasm embraces her and spreads its sweet warmth to Joakim. She trembles and bites her lip in a half-hearted attempt not to disturb the neighbours, which doesn't go very well ...

Joakim looks into Susanne's sensual face, where the mascara is no longer that proper as it was earlier. He enjoys seeing her consumed by lust and longing.

"You couldn't fool anyone; everyone, and I mean absolutely everyone, can see how incredibly horny you are just by catching a glimpse of your face. It's priceless, absolutely fucking priceless!"

He can't tear his eyes away from her and unabashedly savors the sight with his mouth half open as her prolonged orgasm slowly subsides. Before he penetrates her again, she props herself up on her elbow and looks deeply into Joakim's eyes. The previously sensual expression has been replaced by a gentle smile more reminiscent of the Virgin Mary than of a completely horny Susanne. With a voice that fully matches her innocent facial expression, she begins.

"Darling, do you remember when we fantasized about a threesome? I think this is the perfect moment to turn fantasy into reality ..."

The Unexpected Proposal

Wide-eyed, Joakim stares at Susanne. His expression shows that he wouldn't have been more surprised if she had claimed to be a genuine extraterrestrial.

"What are you saying? You mean now, here on the boat?" Joakim exclaims, taken aback.

"Why not? It wasn't long ago that we talked about it, for me it's not just a wild fantasy. It shouldn't be hard to find a horny guy here on the boat. Besides, no one knows who we are; we can fake our names. I can be Carina, and you can be Kjell, or whatever you want. What do you say? Isn't this the right time break the wall?"

He lets Susanne's words sink in and then responds with a voice filled with doubt. "Well ... maybe. But ... we haven't even talked to anyone. If so, how do we do? Should we go down together and to pick someone up, do you have a plan?"

"Of course I have! Here's what I'm thinking: it's probably easier to find a guy than a girl. Guys are always horny and in great need of a fuck, right? The simplest thing would be for you to go down and try to make contact with a suitable guy and ... well, just be straightforward."

"Just be straightforward? You mean I should jump on the first decent-looking guy I see? And then what, simply tell him that I have a horny girl waiting to be properly fucked? Oh yeah, I should also explain that I need help with it. Nah, this doesn't feel right! It sounds a bit crazy. Isn't it better if you go down and pick someone up ... and be straightforward?"

"Well, first I thought so, but it might be hard when I say that my husband is waiting in the cabin ... How do they react? Is there anyone who dares to join then? I think you, as a guy, can explain it better to another guy since we're planning a threesome. It would be different if I were to pick up a guy on my own, just for myself."

"True, but it still doesn't feel like we're planning this together."

"So, you don't think it's a good idea? Should we forget about it?"

After a few seconds of tense silence, Joakim lights up. "You're damn crazy, but thinking about it does get me a little excited. But what if I don't find a guy? I might end up with a woman, how would you feel about that?"

Now it's Susanne's turn to ponder her plan. She falls silent and stares into the large mirror across from the bed. She tries to imagine herself in bed with Joakim and another woman. She struggles to sort out her thoughts and realizes that it's not just guys who needs a proper fuck. The image of herself, Joakim, and a stranger woman in the same bed lingers, even when she closes her eyes. It doesn't feel entirely okay, but she sees something enticing in it. Whatever happens, they have a stable, loving relationship to rely on. It's just sex; she's not looking for a new relationship

Joakim, with his pants halfway up, listens intently to Susanne's response. "I think you should go down to the bar and try to find someone interested in a threesome, preferably a nice guy. If you can't find a guy, you can check out the women, but honestly, I don't know how I would react if you come back with a woman."

"Okay, I'll try to get a guy," Joakim replies thoughtfully.

He puts on the clothes, gives Susanne a quick kiss, and leaves the cabin. He walks slowly, almost in a trance, between the rows of cabin doors. When he reaches the elevator, he hesitates, wondering if he's really about to pick up a sex partner for Susanne.

Thoughts whirl in his mind, and he feels a desperate need to sober up. A few minutes in the chilly air on deck should be enough. Despite saying yes to Susanne's proposal, he is still highly uncertain if it's wise to take the final decisive step. It feels exciting, but how the hell do we handle it if I bring someone she doesn't like? Do we thank the guy for his interest and ask him to leave, or ... does she smiles and bite the bullet?

This isn't easy... and what will be the consequences if she develops a taste for threesomes? I have no idea which scenario is worse ...

After a few minutes in the icy cold on the deck, he decides to at least give it a try. As he reaches the entrance to the nightclub, he subtly pauses for a brief second, takes a deep breath, and steps inside. He heads for the bar and discreetly starts studying the people there in a way he has never done before. Well, checking out guys... doesn't feel quite right. How the hell am I supposed to know who's single and who she finds acceptable? Damn Susanne, she should have taken care of this herself!

Discreetly Joakim scans the guys hanging out at the bar while also looking for a possible single woman. Soon, he discovers that the women without a partner mostly belong to a group of female friends. Disappointed, he realizes that it's probably even harder to get a woman. It seems I have to accept that it'll be a guy if we're going to have a threesome. Well, we did talk about this, so if she wants an extra guy so okay ... Damn, I can't even make up my mind if I like the idea or not. One moment, I'm horny as hell, and the next, it just feels insane ...

Joakim now concentrates his search solely on the male gender. He lets his gaze sweep over a few solo guys at the bar. At first glance, the movie-star-like guy talking to the bartender seems to be the perfect man for the task. But as Joakim gathers himself, he realizes with increasing surprise that the guy obviously has a serious problem with balance. He soon concludes that the handsome man can barely stand up without holding onto something, so he continues his search. The next candidate is a slightly younger guy in tight jeans who appears reasonably sober and genuinely friendly. It's now or never, Joakim thinks, but at that moment, a girl comes and drags the intended target onto the dance floor. It's just to keep looking.

The end result is extremely meager. After thoroughly examining the male clientele, he objectively concludes that the reasonably sober guys who don't look like losers are already taken. The unfortunate ones who haven't managed to find female company for the evening mostly look rather tragic, with their awkward behavior, they would, at best, attract a very desperate woman. After a while, Joakim realizes that the supply of acceptable sex partners is severely limited, he turns back towards the cabin. Despite the disappointing outcome, he doesn't consider the search entirely wasted. Above all, it has been fun to observe people from a completely new perspective. In his focused state, he had almost forgotten the reason behind the search. He desperately hopes that Susanne is still awake and interested in more sex, despite the failed attempt.

The cabin door opens almost as soon as he knocks, he can read both disappointment and relief on her face.

"What happened? Did no one want to or did you not find anyone to ask?" Susanne asks.
Joakim gathers himself and begins to explain. Susanne listens with a tense smile, without interrupting. He finishes

his experience and Susanne's reaction doesn't keep him waiting. He receives a long kiss, and she passionately says,

"I love you so much, especially because you at least tried to fulfill our fantasy."

Despite the unsuccessful attempt at picking someone up, they continue the hot play with feelings that can only be explained by the thought of a third person in bed. All romance is thrown out the window, now there exists only a raw animalistic urge that demands its tribute. Susanne takes a firm grip on Joakim and repeatedly urges him,

"For heaven's sake, fuck me as hard you can."

It's not a conventional lovemaking session; it's more like a battle where both are trying to take control. However, it doesn't last long. After just a few minutes, Susanne writhes in a blissful spasm and futilely pleads with Joakim to calm down. But Joakim doesn't listen; he continues frantically pounding her with vigorous thrusts. The only thing that exists in his consciousness is to unite with Susanne in her orgasmic frenzy, to fill her with the bubbling energy inside him. After a few more seconds, Susanne forgets what she had just asked for. Her first orgasm barely subsides before she is hopelessly lost in a new one. Her lustful cries quickly draw Joakim along, and his violent thrusts gradually transform into convulsive spasms as he finally empties himself deeply inside her with a long, muted moan. It all ends as abruptly as it began. Exhausted, they drift into a dreamless sleep.

Back home in Stockholm, in the car. Susanne starts cautiously. "Maybe it was just as well that you didn't get any hit on your cruising round. I honestly don't know what I would have done if you came back with a guy ... or maybe worse, a woman. In hindsight, in a sober state of mind, you get a different perspective on the whole thing."

"It's probably the same with me," Joakim sighed. "I don't even know how I would have reacted to seeing you with someone else, probably a mix of arousal and jealousy."

In silence, they slowly navigated east in the Stockholm traffic, which, for once, flowed at a decent pace. However, yesterday's tumultuous events were still spinning in Susanne's head. She tried to get some structure on what had actually happened on the boat. Above all, she tried to clarify how she wanted her own and their shared sex life to be in the future.

"Joakim, you know I love you, despite my suggestion. I'm very satisfied with our relationship; you're a good lover, friend, and, not least, a wonderful dad. I really love you!"

"That sounds very nice; flattery is always pleasant, but what do you really mean?"

"Hmm, it's not that easy. But if I put it this way, I can't say that I've completely abandoned the idea of a threesome, but I don't think we should make any more attempts in the near future."

Susanne is silent for a couple of seconds and adds, "But to be honest, I probably don't really know what I mean by the near future ..."

"I understand that; you seem quite eager to have it with two guys, right?"

"I can't deny that, but at the same time, it feels like I'm not quite mature enough for it."

"Maybe we should wait and digest this before moving on. Eventually, if we're still curious, we can maybe connect with some like-minded couple and see if sex with others is our thing. Obviously are both of us a bit hesitant, but who knows, we might like it?"

"Maybe." Susanne replied with a mischievous smile.

"We're probably not alone in these crazy fantasies. Orgies are nothing new, it was popular even among the Romans." Joakim fell silent but continued on the same theme shortly after. "There are probably many people having sex with multiple partners today. Threesomes and group sex are probably much more common than one would think."

Susanne nodded. "You're probably right about what you're saying, but where do we find a guy, or a couple, with the same thoughts as us?" Susanne looked at Joakim questioningly.

"In the past, there were personal ads in men's magazines. That type of ads can surely be found on the internet today, don't you think?"

"Well, there's everything there, but we can discuss this at another time! For now, I think we should put this discussion on hold. Right now, I just feel like getting home and taking it easy. Neither Jens nor Ida has called, but they are adults. They don't need us as much as before, but it would be nice if they could come over for a Sunday dinner?"

"Good idea, we'll tackle the other issue when we've gained some perspective on what happened. Despite our craziness, I think we've had a couple of wonderful days. I love you, you horny thing."

"Ditto," replied Susanne. She closed her eyes and let her thoughts drift into the realm of dreams, where fantasies are allowed to live their own lives, without any moralistic pointers.

Reportage with Consequences

Spring, approximately a year and a half later.

Joakim is enjoying his weekend leave, wrapped in a blan-
ket, warming himself in the pale spring sun that managed
to break through the otherwise dense clouds for the day.
He absentmindedly flips through the paper, he's nearly
done when his eyes catch a headline that reads, "Room
not just for the heart."

The article begins with a reporter overcoming her shy-
ness and conducting an exposé on a swinger's club in
Stockholm. Joakim was unsure of what the term *swingers*
actually meant, other than it being related to sex. However, he quickly found out. The female reporter provided
detailed descriptions of the activities taking place within
the club premises. He hadn't gotten far before he was
completely absorbed by the article's vivid depictions. Despite succumbing to doubt, he questioned its truthfulness.
The story was almost too good to be true. If it had been a
male reporter, I probably wouldn't have believed it.

Evidently, the club was intended for couples who were
open to partner swapping and more liberated forms of
sex. Without any sugarcoating, the reporter recounted
how casual sex happened both here and there in the club.
She also mentioned how she herself became the subject
of a seduction attempt, which she at least claimed to have

rejected. His thoughts turned to Susanne, who unfortunately was at the gym. Intensely pondering how he could get her on board, he concluded that it would be best if she read the article herself. I would be very surprised if she isn't intrigued by the idea; we simply can't miss this.

Susanne had barely taken off her outerwear when he pounced on her. "Come and sit down, you absolutely have to read this. I think you'll like it."

"Oh, really? What's it about? You seem a bit excited."

Excited is an understatement," Joakim replies with a big smile. "I found an interesting article about a couples' club, a club for people who are more open about their sex lives. You have to read it."

She started reading and didn't hesitate to agree with Joakim that it sounded interesting. When she finished, she asked the unnecessary question. "Do you think we should visit the club?" However, she continues without waiting for Joakim's answer. "Sure, it sounds thrilling, but I'm still unsure if porn clubs are my thing?"

"Porn club!" Joakim responds with an unnecessarily loud voice. "It's a couples' club, something completely different!"

"Okay, I understand the difference, but I'm still uncertain if I want to go there. I need some time to think. It doesn't feel very appealing to expose myself more or less naked and have sex in front of strangers. Besides, I feel fat. I've actually gained a few extra pounds."

"I understand you, but I think you're exaggerating about your weight. I don't believe that only people with perfect bodies go to these kinds of clubs. Most likely, they look just like us, some more fit, others in worse shape. I'm not saying we need to decide anything now, but I'm convinced you would enjoy it, my horny darling."

"Yeah, yeah, let's discuss this at a later time. Right now, there are far more pressing priorities we have to take on."

Joakim, struggles to hide his disappointment in Susanne's lack of interest in the world whose existence he had just recently discovered. Nevertheless, he realized the wisdom in not mentioning anything more at the moment; right now, it seemed more important to gather brownie points. He enthusiastically took care of the dishes and spent more time tidying up the kitchen than he usually did. The following evening presented another opportunity. Sunk into the couch, Joakim began with a voice that didn't sound quite like his usual self, despite his efforts. "I was thinking about the article from yesterday."

"Oh," Susanne replied cheerfully. "You mean the one about the demolition site where they want to build a church? No, I understand perfectly what you mean."

"Okay, since you've read the article, don't you think it's something for us?"

"Well, it sounds interesting, but as I said, I'm still unsure. I'm not sure if I'm ready to take that step," Susanne said, and then fell silent. Or am I? Maybe I have only my-self to blame; what Joakim is suggesting is very close to what I proposed on the ferry from Åbo. No, I need time to think this through, he needs to calm down.

Susanne was interrupted by Joakim shortly after. "Come on, I'm sure you would enjoy it! Let's give it a try, if it doesn't feel right, at least we've tried. If it works, it's like accomplishing the otherwise impossible, having your cake and eating it too..."

"I understand, but please, stop preaching!"

"Yes, but think about the advantages. Besides, we won't risk anyone being unfaithful, at least not for a one-night stand," Joakim said with a foolish grin.

"So, we'll be unfaithful at the same time. Is that what you mean?"

"Now you sound like the devil reading the Bible. I just meant that both you and I have ended up in the wrong bed a couple of times, and I think you agree that it was pretty damn awful, right?"

"It was definitely awful, but I'm not sure if that's a convincing argument in this discussion," Susanne replied with a tired tone.

"On the ferry, you were so damn eager for a three-some, but not now. Moreover, this is in a more organized setting, so if we..."

"For God's sake, Joakim, didn't you hear what I said? Stop nagging, drop it! We'll discuss this at another time, got it?"

"Sure, I get it, we'll talk about it when you're ready."

Joakim reluctantly realized that, for the time being, he had to bite the bullet. He would give Susanne the time she needed so that the whole project wouldn't go to hell. Despite knowing that it wasn't entirely hopeless yet, he found it difficult not to show his disappointment. He had to find a way out of this mental impasse, and as an excuse, he decided to go for a jog. However, it didn't turn into a jog; in pure frustration, he ran as fast as he could until he had to slow down. Panting, he continued at a considerably slower pace, sweaty and exhausted. When he arrived home, he noticed with relief that the worst disappointment had subsided. Nevertheless, he couldn't stop thinking about the golden opportunity that would potentially be lost. The next morning, Joakim woke up with the same nagging thoughts he fell asleep to. Susanne's doubts about the excellence of his suggestion had firmly settled in his mind. At breakfast, he cautiously asked if she could at least think about the proposal.

"Yes, I'll think about it, but you have to give me time to figure out what I truly think. I feel the pressure from you all the time."

"Absolutely, you'll have all the time you need, but let's not become retirees before you've made up your mind."

With a heavy sigh and a tired look, Susanne replied, "You'll get an answer, but not right now, you nagging rascal."

They had breakfast in silence, and it wasn't until they got into the car for their previously planned IKEA trip that the mood lightened. The shopping round required them to talk and come to an agreement on the storage furniture they desperately needed. In the end, they settled on a birch veneer wardrobe. The large flat packages were accompanied by the more or less obligatory items such as napkins, candles, and batteries. Despite the occasional lump in his chest, Joakim made an effort not to show his disappointment. The rest of Sunday flowed in a light-hearted atmosphere, and with joint efforts, they managed to assemble the wardrobes. The problem with the somewhat cryptic assembly instructions distracted Joakim from his thoughts, albeit only temporarily.

When evening came, the usually pleasant feeling of getting into bed was absent. Susanne fell asleep quickly, but Joakim couldn't shake off the feeling of unease. He tossed and turned, but the relieving sleep eluded him. The questions pressed on, and once again, he examined himself. How the hell could something that seemed so promising go so wrong? Could I have done things differently? But what if Susanne were to agree to visit the club after all ... is it wise to expose our relationship to something like that? No, this won't work; it only gets more confusing the more I think about it.

The questions piled up, and the few answers he found didn't feel convincing in any way. After endless tossing and turning in bed, he finally dozed off for a few hours. However, the dreamless, deep sleep he had hoped for didn't come; the dreams alternated between regret and anticipation. One second, it was a whirlwind of naked bodies, soon replaced by an icy silence and a frightening feeling of loneliness. The dreams stumbled over each other, and Monday morning arrived, unusually feeling more like a liberator than the feeling of another weekend being over. He buried himself in work, but despite that, the week felt unusually long. He oscillated between hope and despair but managed to keep his promise not to bring up the question again. Without mentioning anything to Susanne, he repeatedly visited the club's website, each time igniting hope, but his solo googling also created a sense of shame. They should have explored the pages together instead. The pictures and information from the club were painfully enticing and stood in stark contrast to the agonizing uncertainty that provided him with no peace. I can't stand this endless waiting; even a no would probably feel better. At least then we could move on based on that ...

Decision Anxiety

Another workweek was coming to an end, Joakim's frustration provided him with no peace, even if it had somewhat subsided. He was increasingly leaning towards demanding an answer from Susanne, but he also realized that he needed to tread carefully. If he pressed her, there was a significant risk that it would result in a definitive distancing. On his way home, he considered stopping to buy a bouquet of roses but realized that he rarely comes home with flowers; the intention would be too obvious.

Even though Susanne seemed unaffected, she was well aware that sooner or later, she would have to reveal her stance. They had been together for too long for her not to notice Joakim's inner turmoil. The question that lingered in a limbo-like state needed to be resolved so they could return to the carefree everyday routine that prevailed before Joakim became aware of the swinger's world. Friday was approaching, and Susanne was convinced that Joakim would bring up the question of the swinger club again.

But ... what do I say when I don't even know what I want? Sure, it sounds exciting, but is it really a good idea to offer your body to a stranger? – Hello, does anyone want to have sex? No, that's probably not how it works, but however it is, the idea is that you should swap partners. And beside of this ... can I handle seeing Joakim have sex with another woman?

Friday evening started as usual, with them putting a little extra effort into dinner, this time a piece of meat from the grill and a mature Bordeaux. Susanne was content to put the challenging week behind her, and Joakim felt more satisfied than he had in a long time. They enjoyed together the tones from Bruce Springsteen's old but wonderful Born to Run album, which effectively washed away the last traces of the workweek. The only thing that disturbed Joakim in the Friday coziness was that a whole week had passed without a single comment from Susanne. Eventually, he couldn't hold it in any longer and cautiously brought up the question. Susanne didn't get angry as he had feared. She sat silently for a moment and then asked a question that gave Joakim a glimmer of hope.

"Do you know where the club is located?"

"Just outside the city center."

"Okay, I'm still not quite clear on my decision, but how do we go on it if we were to visit?"

The star of hope flickered up another notch; Joakim suddenly felt as anticipatory as a child on Christmas Eve. Despite Susanne's positive start, he understood that the proposal was not yet secured. Now it was about navigating carefully between the pitfalls. "It says on their website that you have to contact the webmaster before going there for the first time."

"Oh, they have a website. Why didn't you say anything?"

"Hmm, maybe because a certain person explicitly forbade me from bringing up the subject."

"Whatever, we can check out the site together."

Joakim easily finds the club's website, and Susanne can't help but ask how many times he has visited the site. Somewhat sheepishly, Joakim admits that he has been on the website ten, maybe fifteen times. However, his diligent visits to the site do not prompt any comments. In total silence, they read together the detailed information about the club and its social rules. The page also includes a photo album showing the club and its facilities, though without pictures of any guests. The photos not only display the rooms intended for sex, but there are also pictures of the bar and cafeteria that could be taken at any neighbourhood pub. According to the text, they served beer, wine, and light snacks. There were also pictures of a hot tub, but what drew their biggest interest was undoubtedly the so-called playrooms. Although the pictures only showed empty rooms, their imaginations filled in what the photos left out.

The distinguishing feature of the playrooms was that they were furnished with large mattresses, pillows, and mirrors. The colors, unsurprisingly, were red and black.

Susanne couldn't help but point out that it was strikingly similar to a brothel from an old movie. Before Joakim could protest, she quickly pointed out that she was aware of the difference, that what happened at the club was voluntary, and that no one paid for sex. After clicking through more pages and links, Susanne uttered the decisive words, "When do you think we should go?"

Joakim set down his wine glass with a slight thud. Had he heard correctly? "So, you're willing to try it after all?"

"I think so ... I've been very hesitant, but I think we should give the club a chance. If it's not good, we leave, and if it's the opposite, we'll stay and see what happens. Is that okay for you?

"Absolutely," Joakim quickly replied. "If one of us dose's not like it, we'll go home and forget about it."

At the moment, Joakim was floating on cloud nine, but he still felt the need to solidify what they had just decided. He suggested that they should check the calendar now for a suitable weekend. Susanne flipped through the upcoming weeks. There were many things going on, and besides, Susanne's brother had a milestone birthday. Finally, they settled on a Saturday five weeks ahead, and Joakim's previous disappointment was replaced in an instant by an excited tingling in his groin. Five weeks seemed like an eternity, but it was probably good for Susanne to have time to process her decision.

Spring slowly turned into summer, and the eternity that Joakim had just glimpsed was nearing its end. He was brimming with anticipation, picturing himself and Susanne in a sea of naked people, although he realized it probably wouldn't be like that at all. He still felt highly uncertain about what the swinger world stood for, finding it difficult to detach from the feeling that everything was exaggerated. The positive aspect, however, was that the answer awaited them around the corner, although a few practical details remained. He needed to call the club and get the okay, and they also had to plan how to get there and back.

Despite Susanne not voicing any objections, he was still worried that she might back out at the last moment. A week before their visit, Joakim could breathe a sigh of relief when Susanne confirmed that she still was on board.

She also suggested that they stay in a nearby hotel. "It would be nice if we had some time for ourselves before going to the club. I remember there's a hotel near Solna center, it shouldn't be far from the club."

"Good idea, I'll check and book it tomorrow. Have you told Jens and Ida that we won't be home on Saturday night?"

"I've talked to both of them. I said we were invited to a colleague of yours in Uppsala, and they bought it without question. It's unfortunate to have to lie, but in this case, the truth is worse ..."

"Absolutely, but it's going to be incredibly exciting. Are you nervous?"

"No, not right now, at least. But I'll probably need a couple of glasses of wine before we go. But I agree with you, it's going to be exciting. Believe it or not, this has stirred up the same feelings I had on that trip to Finland. Even though I didn't show it directly, I was very interested as soon as I read the article, but at the same time, I panicked. Before, it was just a fantasy that I had control over, but when it finally depended on me, it wasn't as easy."

"You should know that I appreciate that you eventually said yes, despite still being a bit hesitant. Now we at least get the opportunity to form our own opinion."

"Well, I don't feel that uncertain. I really want to go there and see what it's like. Last Thursday, when you worked late, I read the article again, and apparently, it triggered something. I got so damn horny that I had to masturbate."

"Well, well, now I'm starting to recognize you," Joakim replied, beaming with a broad smile.

"Anyway, since I made up my mind, I've been feeling much better, but we'll stick to what we've said. If it doesn't feel good, we won't stay. Maybe we'll have a glass of wine, but then we'll go back to the hotel."

"Absolutely, we've already agreed on that."

"But Joakim, there are other things we should decide in advance. For example, how far we're willing to go, what we'll do if we come across a couple we like."

"Sounds reasonable. Can you imagine swapping partners if it feels right?"

"I'm not sure," she paused for a few seconds and continued. "I think so, but if either of us has the slightest doubt, we'll skip it."

"Of course." Joakim confirmed with a determined nod.

"I read somewhere that some swingers draw the line at kissing, they think it becomes too personal. Maybe we should adopt that?"

"But does it really matter? Having sex is just as personal, isn't it?"

"Well, yes, having sex is very personal, but kissing is different. I still think we should set a boundary there."

"Alright, if that's how you feel: No kissing if we swap partners. Is there anything else we should consider?"

"That we use condoms if we get that far."

"It's actually unnecessary to mention, it should be obvious," Joakim replied with a sensible expression and continued, "Having rules is good, so we don't argue about such things when we're there."

"Absolutely, but we should still be sensitive and feel it out. Anyway, it's going to be damn exciting to go there ... and see if it's like that reporter claimed."

Heaven or Hell?

The last few days leading up to their club debut dragged on. Time seemed to stand still, the complete opposite of a joyful vacation week that is almost over before it even begins. Despite the arduous wait, Joakim was happier than he had been in a long time. They had the green light from the club and had also found a hotel within walking distance, so at least the practical details were sorted. However, the hardest part remained – to open the door to the world of swingers. What seemed so simple at first no longer felt so obvious; Joakim was torn between exciting fantasies and dark doubts.

Is it the path to an exciting sex life, or will it be like opening Pandora's famous box? Susanne is such a wonderful woman, and I don't want to lose her to some younger horny guy ...

Susanne was also having a hard time. Although the fantasy of a threesome had awakened with renewed energy, she still had her doubts about the decision.

Are we really sane? In the worst case, this could end very badly. Many things could go wrong, but I shouldn't jump to conclusions. Hopefully, it will be an exciting evening.

Finally, they woke up to the long-awaited and at the same time feared day. They couldn't fall back asleep or engage in any morning intimacy. After breakfast, Susanne resumed inventorying her more intimate section of the wardrobe. Disappointingly, she realized that the part of the wardrobe containing the daring outfits needed to be expanded.

"Joakim, I have nothing to wear tonight!"

"Isn't that the point, that we won't be wearing anything? Ha, ha, I get it, but don't you have anything? That black and gold corset is stunning, can't you wear that?"

"Maybe, I'll give it a try."

"Take that and some stay-ups. You have plenty of black thongs."

"Yeah, yeah, I'll try. What about you, what are you going to wear?"

"Hmm, good question. I actually haven't thought much about it."

"I assume you might as well say you haven't thought about it at all?"

"Maybe, but guys usually have an easier time with clothes when we go out for something festive. I'll see if I have some fresh underwear that highlights my best asset and a nice t-shirt. Worst case, I'll have to go shopping right away, or we can do it on the way to the hotel."

With some help from Joakim, the corset and stockings were in place. Susanne examined herself closely in the bedroom mirror. "What you see is what you get," she said with a satisfied smile. Joakim confirmed her assessment with an equally contented smile.

"You look fantastic. I'll have my hands full keeping all the guys away from you, but maybe you don't want that?"

"The whole thing feels quite thrilling, so I can't say in advance what I want or if I want anything at all. How about you, do you feel completely safe with this?"

"Of course not. It's all new to us. We'll take it as it comes and see what happens. Anyway, I'm looking forward to having you in that outfit; you look absolutely stunning."

The day continued to drag on. Joakim took on the task of oiling the deck, something that should have been done much earlier. It wasn't a fun job, but at least it got the clock moving. Susanne also felt the anxiety in her body and went for a jog in the beautiful early summer weather. She enjoyed the exertion and the delicate early greenery along the illuminated trail. The stillness and the soft greenish shimmering light were contagious. The butterflies that had been fluttering around in their stomachs flew away ... although a few stubborn ones remained. The worries for the evening had significantly decreased, and she returned home with a surprising sense of calm.

Joakim had finished the deck, and after a last review of their outfits for the evening, they were finally on their way to the hotel. Once they settled into the room, they headed up to the hotel roof terrace to enjoy the sun and the warmth. June was supposed to be a summer month, and so far, it had lived up to expectations. The forecast promised sunshine, and even the prospects for the evening's adventure looked positive, at least so far. They settled into the sun loungers and unpacked the Greek salad and white wine they had brought.

The terrace turned out to be an excellent vantage point over the surrounding area. They soon discovered that they were not the only ones filled with joy and anticipation. Down on the streets below, the students were celebrating their graduation. The ecstatic and, in some cases, inebriated youngsters paraded in endless processions. There was a spectacular array of more or less imaginative vehicles honking as they passed by. Truck bodies decorated with birch branches and flowers, despite their simplicity, seemed to be the most popular vehicles. The jubilant youths on the trucks sang and hugged to the rhythm of the music, filled with boundless happiness.

After an hour or so the temporary chaos subsided, and a strange silence settled in. However, the youthful party spirit had rubbed off on them. They looked forward to the impending club visit with increasing excitement. Despite their joy, Susanne was plagued by doubts. "Joakim, what are we doing? Are our plans really sensible? What if there are just a bunch of pervert people at the club... that's what worries me the most."

"We'll know later how it is," Joakim replied, giving Susanne a hug. "We can't really back out now; I'm sure we would regret it if we did."

"Of course, we're going to the club; I just get a little nervous when I think about it. Come here and give me something else to think about. Can I check if 'Little Jocke' is prepared for the evening?"

Susanne's hand closed around Joakim's groin. He was quick to respond to the initiative and observed with satisfaction that Susanne had once again forgotten her panties.

"You're wet. Are you getting turned on by fantasies about what might happen tonight?"

Before Susanne could answer, the door to the terrace opened. They continued to kiss innocently but had to suppress their hot feelings for the moment. They returned to the room to get ready for the evening's adventure. After a refreshing shower, Susanne began applying makeup but was interrupted by Joakim, who wasn't quite satisfied with her makeup.

"Isn't that too pale? Shouldn't you add some more eyeshadow and maybe a redder lipstick?"

"I don't want to look like a cheap slut. I might touch it up later, but this will do for now," Susanne replied with determination.

"For my part, I wouldn't mind if you looked a bit slutty. It just turns me on more if you add a little extra around your eyes and wear a really red lipstick."

"You guys are so single-minded and predictable. I think all men are attracted to cheap tricks."

"Well, we're wired that way. Red lips actually remind us of other interesting lips. Just think about bees; they're attracted to the most colorful flowers, so it's not as strange as it seems."

"Yeah, yeah, whatever. I'm almost done. How about you?"

"Yeah, I just need to finish my drink. Did you pack everything we talked about, including the condoms? I put them in just to be safe, you never know."

"It's good to have them handy, but there should be condoms in the playrooms. Are you ready to go?"

On their way, they passed a pub filled exclusively with loud football supporters. Obviously, they were celebrating a victory, on the field or possibly on the streets outside ...

After some hesitation, they squeezed into the crowded venue. They ordered drinks and settled at one of the long tables, the only available seats in the entire pub. It didn't take long before they were engaged in football conversations they didn't quite follow. Surprisingly, they soon realized that the so-called hooligans were harmless and friendly. The conversations soon shifted more towards music than football, which made the discussion much more interesting from Susanne and Joakim's perspective. It felt refreshing to let their thoughts revolve around something other than the impending club visit, even if only for a short while. After a brief but positive experience with the football fans, they excused themselves, citing a waiting party. The guys thanked them for a pleasant chat but also let them know that they had seen through them and the party they were heading to. With an innocent smile, they left the pub and walked slowly the remaining distance to the club.

Nervous and jittery, they tried to determine if the couples ahead of them possibly had the same destination in mind. However, it proved to be a difficult task. Most of them looked too innocent and ordinary, veering off in a different direction than the club. Finally, they spotted a couple where the woman wore a strikingly short skirt and the man sported a pair of stylish tight jeans, but even they veered off before reaching the club. The only couple who eventually disappeared down the basement stairs where the club was expected to be located was dressed quite casually, not even a glimpse of fishnet stockings. Disheartened, they concluded that it was probably impossible to tell from appearances alone if someone was a swinger or not. However, they realized the positive aspect of this, that one's actions and interests didn't necessarily have to be reflected in their appearance or attire.

Shortly after, they themselves descended the same basement stairs, greeted by a solid grey door that gave no hint of the paradise that lay behind it. Joakim questioned if they had come to the right place, but a discreet sign confirmed that they were outside the club; Couples in Hearts. He hesitated for a second but then pressed the doorbell. The door opened immediately, revealing an older gentleman who introduced himself as Preben. He welcomed them with a warm smile, invited them in, and accompanied them to the bar. Behind the counter stood a scantily clad, busty woman. Joakim tried to appear unaffected, but he realized that he hadn't succeeded when Susanne let out a deep theatrical sigh. With a welcoming smile, the alluring lady asked to see their identification and checked them off the list of newcomers for the evening. They exchanged a few words, paid, and received a locker key and a towel in return.

After the registration ritual, Preben returned and offered them a tour of the premises. They gratefully accepted the offer. Although Preben was polite and friendly, his attire was not particularly gentlemanly. Apart from his slippers, he was only wearing a pair of leather string briefs and a matching leather vest. It was still early in the evening, and the activities had not yet fully commenced. Their host assured them that it would be completely different in a couple of hours. Most people would be active around midnight, even the beginners, he added with a smile.

For a brief moment, Joakim drifts away in his imagination, the feeling of having passed through a gateway to another world is palpable. However, his continued thoughts were interrupted by Preben, who told them what the different playrooms were called and which rooms were the most popular ones.

Most of the rooms were very traditional when it came to colors associated with erotica. Red, black, and gold dominated, and all the rooms had a pleasantly dim light. Susanne got the feeling that this must have been what Stockholm's early porn clubs looked like. Some rooms even had mirrors on the walls and ceilings, all to enhance and intensify the guests' experiences. However, the most eye-catching aspect was the oversized mattresses and sofas in the playrooms. The walls were mostly covered with velvet draperies in red or black, occasionally broken up by paintings with erotic motifs. It didn't take much imagination to realize what would later unfold in these rooms. They thanked their guide, who wished them a pleasant evening with a warm smile and a nod that said – I'm sure it'll go well.

On their own, they continued to inspect the different rooms once again. Some were particularly well-equipped, and in one of them, they found a well-used gynaecological chair. Joakim looked at Susanne questioningly.

"Thanks, I had a gynaecological examination a month ago. If I need a follow-up examination, I'll let you know," Susanne replied and quickly moved on.

Another room was dominated by a tall wooden Saint Andrew's Cross, firmly anchored to the wall. The X formed cross was equipped with straps and chains, immediately igniting their imagination. However, both understood that it wasn't a place for beginners. They moved on and stopped by the overcrowded jacuzzi. The couples inside were happily engaged in a discussion while unabashedly exploring each other with their hands. One of the women didn't actively participate in the conversation; instead, she was completely focused on the snorkel that curiously peeked above the water's surface.

The next stop was the darkroom, where it was barely possible to distinguish anything, but the familiar sounds were unmistakable. They stood along the wall until their eyes adjusted to the darkness. They curiously glanced at the couple moaning in the dimness in front of them when suddenly the woman asked if they wanted to join them. Before Joakim could even open his mouth, Susanne excused themselves, saying they needed to change. She took Joakim with her into the light and continued with determined steps toward the changing room. On the way, Joakim suggested that it might be the right place to start.

"You mean the darkroom?" Susanne asked.

"Yes, there we can at least be anonymous."

"Absolutely, it feels like a safe place for beginners. But I think we should focus on having sex by ourselves, next to another couple."

"That sounds great. Let's change and have a glass of wine, then we'll check out the situation in the darkroom. Our locker number is eighteen come on, let's change."

More and more couples kept arriving, evident from the crowded space that served as a wardrobe and changing room. The walls were covered with storage lockers, further reducing the floor space. Despite, or perhaps thanks to, the crowdedness, the atmosphere remained high-spirited. Some of the newly arrived couples looked as uncertain as Susanne and Joakim, but most behaved more confidently. However, it seemed like everyone had the same common desire: To shake off the remnants of the world on the other side of the grey door as soon as possible. With the help of more or less sexy outfits, the guests underwent a very noticeable transformation. Many wore tasteful and sexy dresses, although not everyone succeeded equally well in their choice of clothing. Regardless of style and appearance, it was liberating to see the willingness and courage to showcase their most private sides.

The atmosphere in the changing room was pleasant and lively, indicating high expectations for the evening. No one seemed to have any issues with changing clothes either. Here and there, a naked bottom would peek out as shoes and socks were taken off and put on. Susanne and Joakim were caught up in the positive atmosphere and soon embarked on their own transformation. Despite the presence of unknown people, changing clothes was easy, much easier than they had expected. After the somewhat chaotic minutes in the wardrobe, it felt good to sit at the bar. The white wine cooled pleasantly in their throats, but despite this, Susanne couldn't completely relax. After just a few minutes, she had finished most of her glass and disappeared into the restroom.

The silence in the small space felt liberating, despite the buzzing fluorescent light that occasionally flickered. However, she couldn't help but smile when she realized that the flickering light strongly resembled her own state of mind. Absent and contemplative, she touched up her makeup, applying a darker shade around her eyes and a bright shade of red on her lips. The transformation was striking, she had difficulty recognizing herself in the mirror. Absently, she applied a darker shade around her eyes and an angry red tone to her lips. The transformation was striking, she had difficulty recognizing herself in the mirror. With painful clarity, she realized that the woman staring back at her wasn't as familiar as she had imagined.

Ideally, I'd like to put on my coat and go straight back to the hotel, but Joakim would be so disappointed, and ... probably me too ... Well, somehow it will work out.

During Susanne's restroom visit, Joakim stayed at the bar, discreetly observing the traffic to and from the playrooms. More or less unconsciously, he assessed the women, or more precisely, he noted which ones stirred some extra excitement between his legs. With some disappointment, he realized that many of them were closer to fifty than forty; he had expected a slightly younger crowd. However, after a short while, he changed his mind. His initial judgment was clearly hasty. With growing satisfaction, he saw that many of the women, regardless of age, were truly sexy, especially those around fifty. Many in that age group had that extra something, sensual inviting bodies, and eyes gleaming with anticipation.

Soon enough, he was brought back to reality as Susanne returned. She asked with a mischievous smile, "I understand you missed me, were you bored?"

Joakim didn't seem to catch the sarcasm; her heavier makeup made him momentarily forget about the women he had just been checking out. "You look absolutely wonderful," he replied sincerely. "Not slutty, just sexy and sensual. You're going to get plenty of offers tonight, I'm convinced."

"It's always nice to be appreciated by the opposite sex. The great thing is that it's okay to say no, even though we're at a sex club, or whatever you want to call it. First and foremost, it's about you and me, then we'll see what happens. Have you seen any nice couples, or have you just been eyeing the women?"

"No, not just that, I've also been checking out the couples, but to be honest, I may have looked at the women a bit more," he added with a foolish grin.

"Of course you have. I just wanted to know if you saw any couples where both looked nice."

"I've at least seen two or three attractive couples. I'll let you know if I spot them again."

Suddenly, he lowered his voice. "Take a discreet look behind you; it seems like not everyone understands what kind of club we're at. Aren't that underwear suspiciously similar to a pair of ordinary everyday underwear, except they should have been discarded before the last hundred washes?"

"Yeah, it looks incredibly boring! I couldn't possibly be attracted to a guy like that. Not to mention all those people walking around in washed-out white terry towels. Can they really do that? However, it seems like most of the girls have spruced themselves up a bit; at least you should expect some style."

Joakim brightened up. "Hey, it seems like things are starting to happen."

Susanne fell silent for a few seconds and then responded with a confident voice that didn't quite match the thoughts she had just had a moment ago. "I hear you. Let's take a walk and assess the atmosphere. If it feels good, we can finish off in the darkroom. Does that appeal to you, sir?"

"That sounds absolutely perfect. Finish your drink, and let's go."

Susanne contemplated whether another glass of wine would facilitate what might be awaiting them but realized the advantage of not dulling her judgment with more alcohol. She slid down from the barstool but then hesitated. Damn, a minute ago I was feeling so confident but now… at least my wet panties suggest otherwise.

How well do we know ourselves

They joined the rest of the expectant guests who curiously peeked into the playrooms. Susanne also surveyed the surroundings, but she was more discreet than her excited partner, who more resembled a calf in a green pasture. It was still early in the evening, and there was a disconcerting calmness, but something was happening in the mirror room. Susanne and Joakim joined the curious crowd that eagerly watched the couple who had taken on the role of the evening's first object of desire. In reverent silence, they observed the play on the wide red bed. The woman was on all fours, seductively moving her butt in sync with her diligently working mouth. The man lay comfortably on his back, his gaze fixed on the mirrors on the ceiling, where he could enjoy the play from a bird's-eye view. The growing number of spectators didn't seem to disturb them in any way; rather, they seemed to appreciate all the lustful gazes.

Both Joakim and Susanne couldn't help but feel the increasing erotic sensation. Several of the onlookers were caressing themselves or their partners, and the previously almost complete silence had been replaced by satisfied moans. After a while, two more couples climbed onto the mattresses. Joakim was surprised to see that the incoming couples took positions very close to the first couple.

However, he didn't have to ponder for long why; almost immediately, hands started to gravitate towards the couple in the middle. At first, the newcomers avoided the most intimate parts, clearly, they awaiting some kind of reaction. However, nobody objected, and soon their hands sought more exciting targets. After a short while, the caresses intensified, focusing on the more interesting body parts within reach.

Soon, the participants couldn't possibly get any closer to each other. The men's satisfied groans and the women's short, rapid breath mingled with the buzz of the audience, creating a delightful crescendo. Suddenly, the woman in the middle firmly grabbed the nearest woman's hair and pressed her lips against hers. Without pause, the tongues continued their play until both women united in a loud orgasm. The men persistently continued their rhythmic thrusts until they themselves reached the long-awaited climax. Joakim's arousal intensified by the ongoing orgy, just in an arm's length reach from him. It became too much, he pulled Susanne, suggesting that they join the snake pit.

"No, I'm not going up there," Susanne replied firmly. "We said we would start in the darkroom, and that still stands, right? But I feel the same as you; we can't just stand here and stare all night. Next, the darkroom."

No persuasion was needed. Joakim followed Susanne to the darkroom as faithfully as a male dog follows a female

in heat. They cautiously peeked in and stood to the side
to get an idea of what was happening on the bed in front
of them. At first, the darkness felt dense, and they could-
n't discern any contours or details. However, they immediately sensed they weren't alone as a familiar scent of female sex and a delightful mixture of sighs and moans
filled the air. After a minute, the actors in front of them
became increasingly visible. It was clear that one of the
two couples was nearing the finish line. The woman ar-
dently begged for more until they collectively roared out
their pleasure.

That became the signal for Susanne. She took Joakim's
hand and pulled him down onto the mattress to the left
of the other couple, who were still engaged in some sort
of foreplay. Susanne ended up closest and peered curiously into the darkness. The drapery at the entrance let in
a narrow stream of light, which was enough for her to
discern the outlines of the neighbours, who seemed to be
roughly the same age as themselves. The couple soon left
the foreplay behind. Despite the dimness, she could
clearly see how the woman got on her knees and provocatively pushed her buttocks towards her partner, who immediately complied. In complete silence, he took her by
the hips and penetrated her in a single swift motion. The
silence didn't last long; soon there was an appealing mix
of satisfied moans and guttural groans. Susanne stared
spellbound at the pleasurable spectacle unfolding just an
arm's length away from her.

God, I could easily touch them. Just the proximity makes me so damn horny... but we said we'd keep to ourselves.

Susanne laid down on side, facing the couple next to them. Without averting her gaze from the couple, she directed Joakim's cock to its rightful place. With a satisfied sigh, she pressed her ass firmly against Joakim and gratefully accepted his forceful thrusts. After a while, the neighbours changed positions. The woman slid down on her side, facing Susanne. Both women now lay closely with their faces towards each other. Susanne assumed that the couple wanted to watch as Joakim took her; just the thought made her even more aroused. She closed her eyes and embraced every ounce of pleasure that Joakim generously offered. Susanne flinched when she felt the delicate hand tentatively squeezing her breast.

What is she doing ... surprised realized Susanne it didn't feel any different from when Joakim touched her.

She didn't pull away; instead, she stretched and began gently caressing the woman's partner, but it didn't turn out as she had imagined. With a firm grip, he took Susanne's hand and placed it on his partner's breast. In a mixture of surprise and curiosity, she allowed her hand to passively rest where it landed. Astonished, she noticed how her touch noticeably transformed the breast. The nipple grew like a small flower bud; she buried her fingers in the soft flesh. Joakim watched the women with increasing astonishment and excitement. His increasingly vigorous thrusts brought Susanne even closer to the neighbours. She was now hopelessly lost in the pleasure that was completely taking over her consciousness. The bodies intertwined more and more with each new thrust, and soon the women lay face to face.

The kiss didn't shock her; willingly, she accepted the tongue that seductively found its way between her lips. Her whole body was running wild, she wanted to scream out her pleasure, but the lingering kiss effectively muffled the scream into a soft moan. The unexpected orgasm completely overwhelmed her and immediately infected her temporary partner. For a brief moment, all activity came to a halt, even the men calmed down. However, the interruption was only temporary. Even though the after-effects of the orgasm lingered, she could feel the fingers finding their way into her most susceptible part of her body. For a few seconds, the hand remained completely still, as if waiting for a response, an approval, but Susanne's lustful gasps were answer enough. Soon, the fingers began drawing patterns around her clitoris, starting slowly and gently, then transitioning into caressing, rhythmic movements.

Joakim's teenage erection and the fingers simultaneously vying for access to Susannes most sacred place brought her in rocket speed closer to a new orgasm. Time seemed to stand still, only the present moment existed with a pleasure that totally consumed her. Without releasing the grip of the firm breast, she let her other hand slide downward. She paused only when she distinctly felt that the woman was receiving the same divinely pleasurable treatment that she herself received from Joakim. The intoxicating ecstasy completely took over her consciousness as she felt the smooth, moist sex rhythmically pressing against her hand. In that moment, nothing existed except an ecstatic desire that completely engulfed her. Confused and lost in an ecstatic pleasure, only one thought existed in Susanne's mind; Please, let it never end ...

But nothing lasts forever; suddenly, Susanne was violently pulled back to reality. With a stunning clarity, it dawned on her that she was tightly intertwined with a strange woman. Moreover, between two men who were fucking with all their might, it became too much. She quickly withdrew from Joakim, mumbled an apology, and hastily grabbed her corset on the way out. Before Joakim fully grasped what was happening, she was gone. He apologized the couple and gathered his few garments, stumbling dazedly out to find Susanne.

He found her at the bar. "What happened?

"A good question ... It was just too much, what did I do with that woman?" Susanne replied with a laugh and a slight shake of her head.

"I was very surprised when you two started touching each other. It wasn't that I took offense, just incredibly surprised. You haven't mentioned or hinted that you're interested in women."

"I'm not," Susanne snapped. "I haven't even fantasized about being with a woman, you know what I like! I don't understand what happened. They must have wondered when I just got up and left. I need to talk to her so she doesn't think I got mad or something."

Joakim nodded. "It certainly looked like you enjoyed it, did you?"

"Apparently I did, but I need to think a bit about what that meant. In retrospect, it feels really strange, like my own body betrayed me."

"The agreement not to kiss anyone didn't last very long, or did it not apply to people of the same gender?"

Susanne shrugged. "Everything happened so quickly, and like I just said, I don't really know what..." She was interrupted by a tap on her shoulder. When she turned around, she met the gaze of a friendly, smiling woman in her forties.

"Hi, I'm Eva. I think this is yours," the woman said, holding up an earring. Susanne immediately recognized both the woman and the earring. She nodded in recognition and smiled apologetically. "I understand both where and when I dropped it."

She realized that the dimness of the darkroom didn't provide the anonymity she had hoped for. She asked the woman to sit down, introduced herself and Joakim, apologized again, and explained that her abrupt departure had nothing to do with their company. "It's our first time here, and besides, I've never touched a woman in that way. "It's our first time here, and besides, I've never touched a woman like that. It was quite confusing when I realized what I was doing."

"It's totally okay," Eva replied with a disarming smile and continued, "I remember how nervous I was the first time we were here. My partner and I only had sex with each other, but I think you had a better start, even if it didn't go as planned. You don't have to worry about girl-on-girl action if it's not your thing, just speak up. I wasn't particularly interested at first either. It slowly grew clearer that I appreciated a woman's touch but I still prefer a good fuck." She paused for a moment and continued cheerfully, "But on the other hand, one doesn't exclude the other. Oddly enough, girl-on-girl action seems to come naturally to many women, but for me, it's still just a spice. Many, maybe even most girls in these circles are more or less bi, strange but true."

"Oh," Susanne replied with a pensive expression. "You mean what we were doing in there gets worse over time … or maybe better, however you'll see it?"

Eva smiled. "Something like that, at least it's very common in this world. Well, now I have to go take care of Pelle, my dear partner. Kisses to you, maybe we'll see each other again." Eva gave Susanne a quick hug and hurried away.

Susanne took Joakim's hand and pleaded a bit. "For me, adventures for tonight are enough. I think we should find a secluded corner and end the evening with a really good fuck, just the two of us."

"Sure, darling, it's probably a good idea to take it easy. In my eyes, it's been a very enjoyable evening that has given me a taste for more. How do you feel?"

"It has definitely been interesting and exciting, but despite that, I need to process this."

"I understand."

"But please, before we leave here, you have to fuck me properly."

"Sure, I'll do my very best," Joakim replied with a satisfied smile.

They found a sofa slightly secluded, but after a while, they still had a few onlookers. However, Susanne discovered that it wasn't actually a big problem having people watch, rather the opposite. The thrill of seeing others get turned on by their play only triggered her more. In the midst of the act, she felt a touch on her thigh from one of the spectators. Without hesitation, she removed the caressing hand. It didn't come back.

"That was easy," Susanne whispered. "I hope everyone shows the same respect."

"Forget about it, we have other things to do. You wanted to be thoroughly fucked, and I feel strongly about drowning your wonderful little pussy."

"Yes, darling, drown my cunt in cum."

Determinedly, she digs her angrily red nails into Joakim's pale spring buttocks, and the effect doesn't disappoint. Her plea and sharp nails immediately ensure that Joakim fulfills her wish. A fraction of a second later, she follows him into ecstasy. Satisfied with the conclusion, both realized it was time to leave. Before they left the venue, they paid for the wine and coffee and exchanged a few words with Preben. On their way to the changing room, Joakim was surprised to hear Susanne thank their host confidently, saying,

"We've had a great evening; you'll probably see us again soon."

Despite Susanne's unexpectedly contented evening, she still wrestles with conflicting feelings during the short walk back to the hotel. Her pleasurable play with Eva bewildered her.

Maybe it's as Eva said, that many girls actually are bisexual, and it seems to apply to me too ...

Joakim couldn't help but notice Susanne's thoughtfulness. "You are so quiet? Are you thinking about what happened at the club?"

"Well, yeah, I guess I am, but it's okay. Like I said before, most of it was positive, but I'm still a bit puzzled by what happened in the darkroom."

"Maybe it went a little wrong?"

"No, not wrong at all. I'm mostly surprised at how receptive I was to Eva's invitation."

"It didn't make you feel bad, I hope?"

"No, not at all, but it was definitely a mind-blowing evening. How does it feel for you then?"

"Do you even need to ask?" Joakim replied with a smile. "I feel like we've found our place. It might sound strange, but I actually think this could give our relationship a boost. You should know that I love you for so many things, not least for putting up with my nagging."

"Well, you were really annoying for a while, but now I'm glad you didn't give up. It was good that we tried, and sure, it's possible that this could strengthen our relationship. You didn't get anything extra, but it seems okay anyway?"

"It was completely okay ... actually more than just okay. What happened in the darkroom will keep me going for a while. Now it's easier to wait knowing that we might go back to the club."

"I'm not opposed to going back," Susanne replied and gave Joakim a quick kiss.

Renewed trust in the project

At the hotel, Susanne quickly dozed off, but the memories from the club followed her in her sleep. She woke up early with a tingling sensation between her legs. The experiences from the previous day had turned into a very concrete need in the world of dreams. Under the covers, there lingered a heavy scent of female desire, ready for its male counterpart. Joakim was still fast asleep, but Susanne quickly slipped off her nightgown and crawled next to him. Immediately, she received confirmation that Joakim hadn't been unaffected by the events of the previous day either.

"Uhmm, are you already awake and horny, or did you just want to wake me up?"

"Joakim, I'm really horny! The first thing I thought about when I woke up was what happened yesterday. It's been spinning in my head all night."

"Well, apparently not just in your mind. That scent says a lot about the dreams you've had."

"I've dreamt a lot, but I can't quite remember what," Susanne replied and disappeared under the covers.

Soon, they made love passionately, carried away by a wave of memories from the previous evening. It was a brief and intense encounter that ended with both of them falling back asleep, but this time in a dreamless slumber.

It was close to eleven o'clock when they woke up slightly drowsy, and they both agreed that further activities would have to wait. After a long-shared shower, they felt hungry, but disappointingly, they discovered that the breakfast room had closed for the day. They packed up and headed home.

On the way back, their conversation quickly turned to the experiences of the previous day, and Joakim asked curiously, "Are you still as positive as you were on the way back to the hotel?"

"I think so. It was actually much better than I expected. I guess I had some preconceived notions."

"Okay, so you'd consider going there again, I don't mean right away but maybe in a few weeks?"

"A few weeks ... How's our next weekend?" Susanne giggled.

"Are you kidding? I'm not even sure if I want to go back so soon ... but I think I do."

Both burst into laughter at their childlike enthusiasm, but Susanne quickly became serious. I'm just a little worried about running into someone we know, a neighbour or a coworker. That wouldn't be fun."

"No, that would feel a bit awkward. It would be nice to avoid something like that, but if it were to happen, they would be there for the same reason as us." Said Joakim

"That's a mitigating circumstance. Besides, the risk of that happening is probably not very high."

"I don't think there's anything to worry about. The biggest problem right now seems to be finding a suitable weekend for the next visit," Joakim replied, looking thoughtfully at Susanne.

"We'll take a look at the calendar. If it's not next weekend, we'll at least try to find a slot the following weekend."

"Absolutely, I definitely want to get to know the swinger world a bit better. Something struck me - those odd characters we were worried about were conspicuously absent."

"I was thinking the same thing," Susanne agreed. "Not everyone appealed to me, but no one was extremely strange or unpleasant."

"Actually, it was the opposite. Your lover from the darkroom and everyone else we talked to were very nice and social. Some of them might have been overly so."

"Eva was really nice. By the way, it's good you mentioned her. We need to talk about our rules, especially the one about not kissing others. Yes, kisses are intimate and personal, but in retrospect, it feels a bit ridiculous not to kiss. I vote for loosening that rule. It doesn't mean we have to go around kissing everyone left and right."

"It was you who wanted it that way. Let's just take it as it comes. If it triggers any jealousy or discomfort, we can reconsider our rules."

"Well, our rules …," Susanne laughed. "There isn't much left of them ... except for using condoms. I can't think of anything else at the moment. But it's important that we continue to talk through what happens, especially if one of us is dissatisfied or feeling bad."

"We need to be attentive and make sure we agree on what we do and how far we want to go."

"Anyway, the overall atmosphere was good. Did you notice all the happy laughter in the bar and playrooms? Another thing I noticed was that no one seemed particularly drunk, which I didn't expect." Said Susanne.

"No, me neither. I thought there would be about as much drinking as in a regular bar. Most people seemed to have a pleasant and reasonably sober evening. That was definitely the case for me," Joakim smiled. He didn't receive a response, but Susanne's smile was confirmation enough.

After a late breakfast, or rather an early lunch, Sunday followed its usual course and all too soon gave way to Monday. Back at work, Susanne found it hard not to burst into laughter when she was asked the usual question: How was your weekend?

"It was calm, nothing special," she replied, trying to appear unaffected. She probably succeeded, as no one asked any further questions. The rest of the week went on as usual, except that both Susanne and Joakim found themselves daydreaming more often than usual ...

The next club visit was scheduled for the following Saturday, and they spent Friday evening enjoying each other's company at home. The wine and the sofa soon brought back memories from the club, igniting a desperate need for physical contact. They made love softly and gently; nothing like at the club or the rough fuck in the hotel room. Afterward, they lay entwined, talking about their shared discovery. Susanne tried to explain that she felt both curiosity and worry about their more liberated sex life.

"I think I can handle seeing you with another woman, but if that happens, I need to be close to you. I need to be able to see and touch you. We definitely have to be in the same room," she said.

"Yes, I feel the same way. I don't want to let you go without being able to see you. And I love seeing you enjoy yourself. You look absolutely gorgeous when you're firing on all cylinders." Joakim said with a smile.

With a smile on her lips, Susanne asked perhaps the most unnecessary question. "I assume it's okay for you to swap partners if we find the right couple?"

"It's totally okay, as long as we're in agreement. From what I understand, you're quite eager for a partner swap, maybe with someone of the opposite sex this time?"

"Sure, a little variety would be nice," Susanne giggled, but her tone soon turned serious. "I just get a little worried when I think about our relationship. Things might be moving a bit too fast. If we continue like this every weekend, there's a big risk of losing ourselves."

"Of course, there are risks, but we haven't taken this step because we're tired of each other. In any case, it's probably good to take breaks now and then. We can't go to the club every other weekend."

"It feels good that we're on the same page." She immediately looked a bit happier. "We also need to come up with a good cover story if Jens and Ida ask what we're doing this weekend.

"Even if it gets late, we'll still come home in the evening. We can just say that we're going to dinner at Bengt and Maggan's, that sounds good, right?"

"Okay, let's go with Bengt and Maggan. Another lie, but unfortunately, we'll probably have to get used to lying to our children."

"Yeah, it feels a bit off, but do we really have a choice?"

"No, it's the only feasible option. We'll have to continue coming up with credible excuses, but I suppose they can still be considered white lies, right?"

Before their club visit on Saturday, Joakim offered to abstain from alcohol in an attempt to appear as casual as possible. "If I'm sober, we can take the car, and I can perform better too. I know you like it when I'm on my game." He added hesitantly, "And maybe other women appreciate it too ..."
"It's definitely good that you're steadfast, and I might ... even enjoy if you bring some joy to a fellow woman."

Both of them felt much more secure about this club visit. Although they still had a multitude of unanswered questions and thoughts, the concerns that troubled them during their first visit no longer bothered them. Memories from the previous weekend awakened during the short walk from the parking lot to the club venue. A pleasant anticipation spread through their bodies, pushing away any lingering doubts. The hesitations they had last Saturday were gone, and even the grey door felt more welcoming than intimidating this time.

They rang the bell, but this time it wasn't Preben who opened the door. Instead, a busty blonde woman in a leather corset greeted them. Joakim nodded and smiled, though he would have liked to pay her a compliment.

Susanne couldn't help but smile at Joakim's awkward reaction. "I understand that you were a bit speechless; she was quite stunning."

After changing in the locker room, they took a tour of the playrooms. They were empty, but it was still early in the evening. They settled down at the bar. The couple behind the counter, who were also the hosts for the evening, turned out to be friendly and easy to talk to. Soon, a lively discussion ensued, and the hosting couple proved to be a wealth of knowledge about the club and the swinger lifestyle in general. Willingly, they shared their many years of experience in the swinger world. After an intense conversation, Susanne happily noted that they had far fewer unanswered questions than when they walked through the door. The crash course in swinger knowledge eventually came to an end, and they thanked the hosting couple for the pleasant conversation before returning to the playrooms. By now, more guests had arrived, and they made their way to the mirror room. However, this time the mattresses were empty, and Susanne chose a smaller sofa instead of the large bed.

"I think we should start on our own. If it feels good, we can continue somewhere with more space. Is that okay?"

As confirmation, Joakim took off his underwear. They started cautiously but soon became more daring. Several couples passed by, some stopped and watched, but no one tried to join their play. It was a quick encounter, and they realized that making love in front of others wasn't a big issue. Afterward, they returned to the bar, had some coffee, and engaged in further conversation with the hosting couple. Joakim suggested they check out the darkroom.

Susanne nodded thoughtfully. "The darkroom sounds good. You never know what might happen there. The chance, or I should say the opportunity of meeting the same couple as last time is probably not very high," she smirked mischievously.

However, the darkroom was completely empty. They positioned themselves in the middle of the wide bed and began caressing each other. Before they could progress much further, they were joined by a couple who apparently had no need for foreplay. The man barely had time to lie down before his partner started riding him. After just a minute or so, their hands wandered towards Susanne and Joakim, who didn't object. Instead, they cautiously reciprocated with increasingly intimate caresses. Joakim prepared to penetrate Susanne but was interrupted by a sensual voice. "How about a partner swap?"

Joakim looked questioningly at Susanne, and the answer came quickly. "I'm up for it, and I guess you are too."

Joakim nodded happily and retrieved a condom, but then they encountered a struggle. It wasn't easy to open the condom package with sticky fingers, but with some persistence, the condom finally ended up in his hand. However, the struggle to open the package took a toll on his erection, so he needed to regain his momentum. The other man was evidently more comfortable with the situation and was already engaged with Susanne. Despite the darkness, Joakim couldn't help but notice that she was enjoying herself tremendously, evoking a peculiar mix of arousal and jealousy.

There wasn't time for deeper contemplation; his temporary partner demanded attention. The issue with his erection was resolved with a bit of oral sex, and soon there was something to wear the condom on. The thin rubber membrane reduced some of the sensation, but it was more than compensated by the enthusiastic response he received from the woman whose name he didn't even know.

While he enjoyed Susanne's increasingly rapid breathing, the woman in his arms expressed her appreciation with enthusiastic yes, yes for each new stroke. Eventually, it became too much, and Susanne's moans indicated that she was unmistakably approaching climax, demanding her tribute. Joakim's pleasurable groans quickly infected his partner, who loudly shared her satisfaction.

The moans slowly faded, and all parties involved relaxed in contentment for a brief moment. Joakim's temporary lover introduced herself and her partner as Lena and Kjell from the heart of Södermalm. Lena sighed contentedly and added, "That was a great suggestion, don't you think?"

Both Susanne and Joakim immediately agreed with the statement, and after a little small talk about the club, Kjell asked if they were part of any online forums?

"No," Joakim replied somewhat apologetically. "We're beginners; this is only our second time here. We haven't explored any web forums yet, but I suppose there are plenty of those?"

Kjell laughed heartily at Joakim's lack of knowledge. "Oh yes, there is a plethora of such websites." He explained that they themselves were on Bodycontact,

Sweden's largest contact site for swingers. "Primarily to stay in touch with our swinger friends. Of course, there are some unreliable individuals who aren't always what they claim to be, so you have to be cautious. But overall, it works quite well, and it's a free service."

"Oh, Bodycontact, we'll check it out tomorrow, but for now, you can have our Hotmail address so we can maybe meet again another time."

"Absolutely, we come here once or twice a month, so we'll probably see each other again. We'd love to do this again," Lena said, giving Joakim a kiss on the cheek.

"Ditto," agreed Susanne. "It was really enjoyable, and I'm sure my husband agrees with me, right, darling? Let's go to the bar and write down our email addresses."

They exchanged addresses and chatted for a while, but the clock was approaching two. Although things were still happening in the playrooms, the crowd had significantly thinned out, and it was enough for this time.

On the way home, Susanne made an attempt to summarize the evening. "Our first visit turned out very differently from what I had imagined, but it was still an exciting and pleasant evening. And tonight... well, it actually turned out even better. Lena and Kjell were really nice, both inside and outside the playroom. I really hope we meet them again."

"Works for me," Joakim replied. "But it's a funny world we've stumbled into. Did you think about how we

started with having sex, and then we introduced ourselves, not quite the usual order."

"Yeah, a little bit odd; but anyway, I can't say I have
any problem with introducing myself afterwards," Susanne said with a big smile.

"No, it's not a problem for me either. It seems we
both agree to continue with this. Are we already hooked
after just two times?"

"It seems so, but we might encounter worse things
than that," Susanne replied with a meaningful look.

Both agreed that it was a smart move for Joakim to abstain from alcohol. First and foremost, everything worked
perfectly fine, except for the condom mishap. Having access to the car was also a big plus. Joakim realized that
even a good wine paled in comparison to the obvious
benefits of abstaining from alcohol. On Sunday evening,
they had time to Google the contact site that Lena and
Kjell had recommended. They were very curious about
what Bodycontact had to offer and were pleased to find
that the site seemed reliable.

They immediately started creating a profile but quickly
encountered the first obstacle. What should they call
themselves, what nickname should they choose? They
settled on Sussi&Jocke initially but soon changed their
minds, finding the names too revealing. After tossing
around some more suggestions, they decided that Susanne would use the name Cissi in these contexts. Thus,

their nickname on the contact site became Cissi&Jocke. But choosing the nickname was just the beginning; there was still much left to complete the profile. They had to fill in details about age, gender, sexual orientation, height, weight, etc. They were also expected to provide a brief description of their personality and what they liked, both in and out of the bedroom.

Susanne sighed, "This isn't easy. Gender and age are straightforward, but stating what we like in bed is a bit trickier. After these club visits, I'm far from certain about what I like or dislike. It seems like we have sides to us that we weren't even aware of or dared to explore before."

"That does feel both exciting and a little scary," Joakim said, running his fingers through his hair in frustration. "Well, let's start by writing down what we do know or at least what we think we know. Maybe we can get some tips on how to phrase it by looking at other profiles."

"Getting tips and ideas shouldn't be a problem. There must be thousands of members on this site alone. This way of socializing seems to be more common than we thought."

"Yeah, apparently," Joakim replied, immediately clicking through a dozen profiles. "Almost everyone has pictures in their profiles. Maybe we should add some of our own? That way, nobody has to buy a pig in a poke, so to speak."

Joakim nodded. "Absolutely, we can take some pictures one evening during the week, but no face pictures."

"No, definitely no face pictures. Maybe I can wear a hat or hide my face with hair or something. I'll put on something sexy and try to look a bit seductive, but I'm not going to expose myself like some people do. Some pictures are downright tasteless, taken during a gynecologically examination or something! It's just distasteful, not sexy in any way."

"Exactly, it should have some style and finesse. Besides, explicit genital pictures don't say anything about the person otherwise. We should also take some pictures of me, but from a distance. We don't want too much focus on the penis."

"No close-ups, but you should definitely show that you have a nice cock."

A few days later, when they uploaded the pictures, they were surprised to see that their profile had already received nearly two hundred visitors, and there was a notification of a message in their inbox.

"Susanne, if you feel for an extra guy, you have the opportunity. A guy, our age says he can anytime."

"For now, I'll get what I need at the club. Decline, but do it kindly."

The next club visit was scheduled for the following Saturday, and everything seemed fine. But on Thursday, disaster struck with full force. Susanne got her period. The club visit was replaced by a much less sexy activity, a trip to the cinema. The movie was enjoyable, but Joakim couldn't help feeling that life was unfair, and unsurprisingly, he received wholehearted agreement from Susanne. The next possible opportunity was two weeks away, a significant period of time in their eyes, but they had to bite the bullet.

Beginners vs. Veterans

After a couple of unusually long weeks, they are once again on their way to the club. For the third time, they stand outside the grey door. Expectations are high, but after a round in the playrooms, they disappointingly conclude that the few couples there do not in any way raise the pulse. They spend the evening together and seriously consider leaving after a social moment with the host couple at the bar. They pay for their drinks and are on their way to the changing room when another couple arrives, a couple that immediately catches their attention.

"Check them out," Joakim whispers and follows the couple with his eyes as they disappear towards the playrooms.

"Why not, both of them look hot. They seem to be in a hurry. Should we join them and see what they're up to?"

"Absolutely, if they get started, we can get fairly close and see what happens."

The couple was indeed in a hurry; they are already having sex, and the position they have chosen with the woman on top offers a pleasant sight. Susanne quickly kicks off her shoes and lies down a few meters away from the man, who smiles and waves invitingly. They immediately move a bit closer, and as soon as Susanne is within reach, a strong hand grabs her breast. Joakim follows and gently begins to caress the ass that sways seductively next to him, and the result is not long in coming. The woman immediately suggests a change of partner as if it were the most natural thing in the world.

Before Joakim even opens his mouth, he hears Susanne's happy voice, "Okay, honey, why not?" A second later, she is on her way over to the couple.

Joakim, however, has no objections; he welcomes the woman who has now made the corresponding move. No time is wasted as she eagerly takes care of Joakim's awaiting erection. Without releasing her prize, she makes a less successful attempt at introducing herself. Joakim catches something that sounds like Therese and possibly Janne, which later turns out to be true.

After the intense start, they continue at the same rapid pace. Joakim doesn't need to ponder for long to know that Susanne is doing well; her loud yes, yes mantra says it all.

However, he is not as quick in the turns, and while he struggles with the condom, Therese asks an unexpected question, "Which hole do you prefer, the large or the small one?"

Decision anxiety hits him like a ton of bricks, and the answer becomes a clumsy grin and a "Well... that's a damn good question ..."

After a second of contemplation, he decides to start with the ordinary way. He thoroughly enjoys Therese's intense response, but he can't quite let go of the question he was just asked. Curiosity and desire take over, and he suggests switching to the backdoor.

"Absolutely, you're welcome wherever you want," Therese cheerfully replies.

Suddenly, reality catches up with him. The unfamiliar situation and the late hour take their toll, and his erection falters. Neither he nor his temporary partner can remedy the situation, and he eventually gives up with a heavy sigh. He apologizes for his diminishing erection and sees with some satisfaction that Janne is also having trouble with his erection.

However, Therese doesn't take his failure too hard and offers some comfort. "Well, well, these things happen. We can continue where we left off next time we meet. We're often here, actually too often, so we'll probably see each other again soon."

"That would be nice," Joakim replies rapidly.

Susanne adding, "Are you on Bodycontact or any other site?"

"Oh yes, we're on BC, among others," Therese answers.

They exchange nicknames and chat for a while before parting ways. It's approaching three o'clock, so it's time to jump in the shower and get ready to head home, and as usual, a lively discussion about the evening's events ensues.

Susanne smiles and shake her head. "What a couple! They were wild, but fun. I'd love to meet them again."

"Absolutely, I have something to finish with Therese. Maybe you didn't hear what she asked me?"

"Well, not really. I guess was a bit preoccupied with other things at that moment."

"She asked if I wanted to fuck her in the big or the small hole ..."

"There you go, and which hole did you choose?" Susanne asks with a curious expression.

"I was a bit taken aback and was very traditional. It's just that I regretted it after a while, but then I had difficulty getting a good hard-on. It didn't work, neither back nor front. It didn't quite turn out as I wished, but anyway, she was wonderfully wild and spontaneous."

Yes, yes, it's important to choose wisely ... right from the start. Janne was probably just as wild, but he made the same initial choice as you. He fucked me so damn hard; it was almost painful but at the same time damn good. For a while, I really thought I was going to explode."

"Well, it turned out to be a successful evening in the end, despite not much happening before they showed up. Now, let's get going and head home."

After frequent visits to the club in Solna over the summer, they feel comfortable in the swinger environment and are looking for new challenges. After a tip and some googling, they discover Club Adam and Eva in Norrkoping, which presents itself as an organized and reputable club.

"Exciting to try out a new place," says Susanne as she curiously clicks through the website pages.

"Well, it looks good, but as usual, it depends on who's there for the evening."

"In Solna, we haven't had to deal with any real idiots, so I hope it's the same friendly clientele in Norrkoping."

"It's probably the same there, just ordinary, normal people looking for some cozy moments and good sex."

With a worried frown, Susanne shakes her head quietly. "I still worry from time to time that our children or someone we know will find out what we're doing. Jens would probably just shrug it off, but I think Ida would be really upset. And what do you think my brother or my colleagues at work would say? They would freak out."

Joakim also looks briefly concerned but quickly brightens up. "Sure, there might be a fuss, but the storm would probably blow over pretty quickly."

"Hopefully, you're right, but being a woman, I know how women think. Some of my coworkers would probably openly distance themselves, maybe even stop talking to me, although some would probably be jealous of our exciting life."

"Are women really that petty?"

"Well, I might be painting the worst-case scenario, but sometimes I think some actually deserve to be called bitter cunts. The tragic thing is that the reason behind often is a boring or a mean man at home."

"That's sad, but you're probably right in what you're saying," Joakim sighs.

With a worried tone, Susanne continues, "When it comes to Jens and Ida, we would have to explain how it is, that we're not just sleeping around with anyone. We're adults and have control over our own sex lives, but I'm still worried, maybe mostly about how Ida would react."

"It's probably not a problem as long as we continue to be discreet and think about what we say and do. We need to make sure not to leave any traces, clear the browsing history on the computer after visiting club websites and such. The same goes for the camera, not keeping questionable pictures on the memory card."

"You're right, as long as we're cautious, no one needs to find out anything," Susanne replies, and the frown between her eyes smooths out. "Hmm, just talking about it seems to have calmed me down. I think we should give the club in Norrkoping a chance, maybe it's as good there as our home club?"

New club, new experiences

A couple of weeks later in Norrkoping ...

The first thing in Norrköping is to find the club's location. It turns out that the club is only a stone's throw from the harbour. The area gives a dubious impression which is further enhanced by the aging Polish cargo ship at the dock. It has clearly seen better days, the rust covering large areas seems to be well on its way to winning the battle. Undoubtedly, it is in dire need of a steady captain who could revive the long overdue maintenance. The whole environment is in stark contrast to the pictures they saw on the club's website; hopefully the external and internal environment are two different worlds ...

After checking into the hotel and getting ready, they take the short walk to the club. Soon, they find themselves in front of another grey basement door. However, there's no need to wait to be let in; they can just step inside. They are greeted with a cheerful "welcome, have you been here before?" The friendly reception calms them down, and they quickly take care of the practical arrangements and change into suitable club attire. Both of them are excited and find it hard to hide their curiosity as they begin their inspection tour. They happily note that the website's pictures match reality. The decor and colors bear a strong resemblance to the club in Solna, but the layout of the playrooms is slightly different.

It's still early in the evening, so they have plenty of time to explore the premises before the buffet is served. With growing satisfaction, they observe that the rooms look pleasant and inviting, and there are some details they haven't encountered before. One of them is a room with bars that can be locked from the inside for those who want to be alone but still allow others to watch. Another room or rather feature that they don't recognize from Solna is a narrow, elongated room with several round holes cut out in the wall, both high and low.

The room facing the nearest playroom immediately piques Susanne's interest. "It doesn't take much imagination to envision what could stick out through those holes..." she giggles.

"I understand that imagination can run wild, but did you see the room next to it? It was much larger than the biggest playroom at our home club. If it's full, there will be quite a crowd; we should take a look in there later," says Joakim.

"Come on, I see they're starting to set up the buffet. If we hurry, maybe we can choose our table neighbours," says Susanne, pulling Joakim along.

They end up sitting across from a friendly couple from Norrkoping, Karin and Magnus. Karin soon leads the conversation to their favourite vacation destination, a

French naturist paradise on the Mediterranean coast. Magnus explains that they have spent the past seven vacations in a wonderful place called Cap d'Agde.

With enthusiasm, Karin adds that the experiences there are undeniably addictive. Magnus nods in agreement and sighs, "One downside of constantly traveling there is that it's becoming difficult to come up with believable excuses. Our relatives, especially my sister, are a bit suspicious. She thinks it's strange that we insist on vacationing in France year after year."

"We can't stop going there, though. Let our relatives believe what they want," Karin adds.

The pair continued to convey a seductively alluring image. According to Karin and Magnus, Cap d'Agde, or simply Cap as it is usually called, is the closest paradise you can get on earth. The area is fenced and includes several swingers' clubs. In addition, there is a wide range of restaurants and various shops. In short, everything you need. "Really, there's absolutely no reason to leave the area if you don't necessarily want to.

Both Susanne and Joakim are soon completely absorbed in the vivid description. At the moment, they have completely forgotten the real reason they are in Norrkoping and just want to hear more about this fantastic place.

"So, during the day, everyone lies naked on the beach... and only young beautiful people like us? " Susanne wonders with a telling smile.

Karin quickly responds, "If you mean regular people like us, then yes, that's accurate. In that regard, it's no different from a regular vacation destination. There are all kinds of people, slim, thick, old, and young. Of course, you can find a few gods and goddesses with perfect bodies, but most of us have figures that may have passed their expiration date. "

"But not everyone can be swingers, right? " Susanne continues.

"No, not at all," Karin adds. "I would guess that barely half are swingers. Most are just regular naturists or possibly swinger wannabes. Especially the hardcore faction of naturists keeps to themselves and are careful not to mix with people like us. Many naturists also bring their children, so there's a clear division of the beach ... which is a good thing.'

"Okay, and how is it divided?" Susanne asks curiously.

Magnus takes over where Karin left off. "When you leave your accommodation, you come to the first part, the family beach as we call it. It's peaceful there, no sex at all, but everyone, except maybe one or another shy teenager are naked. After the family section, there's a strip of beach, a sort of no-man's-land where beach umbrellas are usually scattered sparsely. Then comes the part of the beach we love, the swinger beach. It's much more crowded there, sometimes it's even difficult to make your way to the water without stepping on someone's towel. During the day, it's usually quite calm, although it heats up now and then. By the way, sex on the beach is not allowed. The police conduct occasional raids, and if you're caught in the act, you'll end up in jail with hefty fines."

"Wow, how much?" Joakim asks, his voice tinged with concern.

"I've heard a figure of fifteen thousand."

"Really?"

"And that's in euros ... " Magnus added

Joakim looked at Magnus with raised eyebrows "Are you kidding?"

"No, and not only that, if you're convicted as a sex offender, you could end up in prison for up to 1 year."

"Damn, does anyone even dare to engage in sex on the beach? "

Magnus kept on. "I haven't seen or heard of the police catching anyone for sexual activities on the beach, so the risk is probably not very high if you're cautious. However, you should be careful. The French authorities don't hold back and can be tough if they see a reason to intervene. Thankfully, you rarely see any police on the actual beach. Usually, they do their job from the lifeguard hut, which is located on a small hill around where the swinger beach begins. When they are on duty, you should definitely be cautious."

Karin interrupted Magnus. "But thankfully, they always leave early in the evening, and that's when things start to happen." Karin says with an infectious laugh.

"Then it's enough to keep calm until the evening," Joakim says, looking relieved. "At least it doesn't seem difficult to find the right part of the beach."

Karin nods and continues her fascinating story. "It's nearly impossible to miss the swinger section. If you somehow manage to do that, you'll soon come to the area where the gay guys hang out. It's mostly guys between twenty and eighty, but also lesbian couples and she-males."

Both Susanne and Joakim had an endless stream of questions about accommodations, clubs, the best way to get there, and so on.

"How are the clubs?" Joakim asks, "I imagine they're bigger and more luxurious than our Swedish clubs?"

Magnus ponders for a moment before answering, "Well, many of them are probably both bigger and more extravagant than the clubs back home. The largest club within the gates is probably Glamour; I would estimate that they allow around three hundred people per night during the peak season. Another one of the bigger and more popular clubs is Extasia, but it's not located within the area; it's about twenty kilometres north of Cap."

"Okay, but how do you get there if you don't have a car?" Joakim wonders.

"If you don't have your own car, you can often share a taxi or a minibus with others heading there. It's a nice club, and usually, you start with some food along with a reasonably serious performance during dinner. But the best part is that there are playrooms both indoors and outdoors. One of the more interesting outdoor facilities is something we jokingly call 'the smorgasbord.' It's basically just a large round bed at waist height where the girls lie down while the guys stand at the sides. It works really well," Magnus adds with a satisfied smile and continues, "There are often quite a few Frenchmen there; Karin loves the club. Language can be a problem, but even if you're not fluent in French, the conversation usually works out in a pleasant way."

Susanne continues bombarding them with questions. "How many clubs are there in the naturist area? Are they only for couples, or do they also allow single guys?"

Karin looks dreamy as she answers, "Yes, there are quite a few, maybe not ten, but not far from it. Most of them also allow single guys."

Joakim apologizes for their curiosity but finds it hard to stop. France feels more and more like their next vacation destination, leaving Thailand in the dust. "When is the best time to travel there, during the high season?" Joakim asks curiously.

Karin responds immediately, "I have a weakness for French men; they really show their appreciation for women. Typically, we travel down during the French holiday period, which starts at the end of July and extends into the later part of August."

"But then there must be thousands of swingers there??" Susanne replies, wide-eyed.

"Absolutely", Karin answered. "It's quite crowded during the high season, both on the beach and at the clubs. There are about thirty thousand bed spaces in the area, but it can still be difficult to find accommodation during that period if you haven't booked well in advance."

"Thirty thousand ... and you say nearly half of them are swingers, that sounds unbelievable," Susanne says, amazed.

"It's not an exaggeration to say that it gets busy. We've been there earlier in the season too, and it's good then as well, a bit less hectic, but from my perspective, there aren't enough Frenchmen."

Susanne asks Karin to describe a typical evening in Cap, and she doesn't need to be asked twice. She starts with a happy smile. "I don't think you can say there are any typical evenings; something unexpected usually happens in a positive way. If we're going to a club or meeting another couple, we often start at one of the restaurants or bars in Port Nature. It's so nice to just sit there and see all the crazy and alluring outfits; you can practically see anything. And when I say anything, I really mean it. Even if you think you've seen it all, you still raise your eyebrows occasionally."

"All right, so Port Nature is the spot where you go out to eat and put yourself on display, if you're into that?"

"Yes, there are several good restaurants there, and if you continue toward Port Ambonne, which picks up where Port Nature ends, there are more. The idea of exposing oneself may sound strange, but I believe many, especially us women, have an inherent need to challenge our surroundings." She pauses for a few seconds and adds, "I think there's a little exhibitionist in most women, don't you? Over time, I've realized that I belong in that category myself. I really enjoy being noticed, at least in these kinds of contexts. Often is it enough to put on a sexy dress to get me wet, even if I'm alone at home." She concludes with a contented sigh.

"I understand completely," Susanne interjects, smiling in recognition.

Susanne and Joakim look at each other and nod; they wholeheartedly agree on where to spend next year's holiday.

"It's been really nice talking to you guys; thank you so much for putting up with all our questions. Who knows, maybe we'll run into each other in Cap next summer," Susanne says.

Joakim nods in agreement, he hugs Karin and excuses himself. "But now; let's see what's happening in the playrooms."

The room with the giant mattresses is next on the agenda, and it's far from full. Susanne chooses a spot near the wall with the intriguing openings or *glory holes*, as Karin called them. They lay out their towels and sink into the soft mattress. The conversation they just had with Karin and Magnus has distracted their thoughts; now it's time to refocus on sex. Susanne energetically takes on the task of arousing the one-eyed snake. Soon she's able to straddle Joakim, she rides him slowly while scanning the other couples in the room, maybe some to play with?

Suddenly she gets a very concrete indication of how to use a glory holes, a proud cock emerges eagerly from the hole closest to her. She stares at it in fascination for a few seconds before reaching out and letting her hand close around the demanding, erect cock. Nothing strange, just a completely natural reflex. Soon another stiff cock appears within reach. In less than thirty seconds she has two magnificent cocks in her care. With a satisfied smile, she jerks off both treasures rhythmically and firmly. After a short while, she increases the pace for the first visitor. Contentedly, she notices that the thin wall does not significantly dampen the man's satisfying grunts. Her intense efforts soon yield results. The man presses himself hard against the wall, which creaks alarmingly but holds. Satisfied, she hears how the unknown man on the other side moans as the sperm spills over her hand. She eases her movements, squeezing and stroking until the hardness subsides. She takes care of the last drops and shifts her attention to the still hard and yearning cock. Determined, she squeezes and releases the balls as she jerks the man harder and harder. Just seconds later, she gets her payback. The man behind the wall moans hoarsely as he spreads his load over her breasts in heavy spurts.

Joakim, who was initially curious and aroused by Susanne's initiative, now feels completely forgotten. Susanne barely has time to finish her private crusade before Joakim grumbles in an attempt to appear firm and demanding.

"You horny thing, I'm actually next in line and this time I set the rules. Use hands and mouth, no pussy. And remember… you are not allowed to touch yourself until I'm satisfied, is that clear?"

Susanne immediately gets on board, saying, "Yes, sir, I'll do my very best."

Joakim lights up, pleased to have her undivided attention again. Susanne also enjoys the game and the unexpected turn of events. With enthusiasm, she carries out the command, and soon her efforts bear fruit. Joakim's expressive body language leaves no room for misinterpretation. Quickly, but not quite quick enough, she dives down to receive the awaited reward. But Joakim is clumsy, and most of the coveted fluid ends up in her hair. Afterwards, despite Joakim's lack of precision, Susanne giggles contentedly.

"What a start ... I was completely swept away of the things popping out from the wall and then ... "

Joakim smiled. "I believe everyone in the room noticed that."

Susanne returned the smile. "Anyway, afterwards; I got
so dam horny when you were playing, transforming my
behaviour to disobedience. Or maybe it wasn't just a
game? Perhaps you were actually a little jealous?"

"Well, maybe a little bit, but most of it was actually just
play."

Susanne smiles mischievously, "But Joakim, I didn't
reach the peak. You actually owe me an orgasm."

"Oh, don't worry, I'll make sure you're satisfied, but
first, I need a break, and maybe you do too?"

"Absolutely, but first and foremost, I need a shower.
Three loads of cum in less than fifteen minutes leave
their mark ..."

From the couch next to the bar, they discreetly observe the couples and single guys hanging around the
counter. Five single men and four couples. Three of the
single men are slightly overweight, worn out, and greying,
not exactly dream princes. The other two, however, look
genuinely nice. Susanne hopes intensely that it was these
two who had the pleasure of her attentions at the glory
hole wall.

The couples at the bar have a similar range, two fresh
and dressed up, while the others haven't dressed up or
made any effort to enhance their appearance. They seem
both unsure and out of place. One couple engages in a

whispered conversation, and the woman who gets up pulls at the man, but he doesn't budge. Eventually, she apparently decides to seek her own adventure, spinning around on her heels and disappearing in the direction of the playrooms. The man stays behind, sighs in resignation, and orders another beer.

After replenishing their fluid reserves and feeling satisfied with the clientele around the bar, they continue their journey. The first thing that catches their attention is a few couples peeking curiously behind a curtain. Above the entrance sign, it says Movie Room, but a large sign next to it advertises something much more interesting: Doctor Pelle's Spanking and Caressing Workshop.

They sneak in and join the curious crowd that eagerly watches the woman whom Pelle alternately caresses and massages. Her entire body glistens with massage oil, and Pelle's efforts have clearly had the intended effect. She trembles and practically levitates from the massage table when she finally reaches her destination with an extended moan. With the support of her partner, she leaves the table, and Doctor Pelle immediately looks around for someone in urgent need of a pleasurable treatment. He loudly proclaims his skills, giving Susanne a suggestive look, but she just smiles and shakes her head in denial. However, a second later, her spontaneous side takes over. Suddenly, Joakim hears a "Well, why not."

She jumps up on the table, takes off her boots, and turns to Joakim, saying, "Darling, you'll keep an eye on me, won't you?"

Surprised by Susanne's change of heart, he helps her free herself from the corset and whispers, "I'm here if you change your mind. For me, it's completely okay. You know; I love watching your face turning into mad pleasure."

They are soon interrupted by Pelle, who rudely holds up a pair of worn leather cuffs and points to Susanne's hands. Gently but firmly, he fastens the cuffs around her wrists and then attaches the carabiners to the massage table. Locked and vulnerable, she gives Joakim a smile before closing her eyes and waiting for what to comes next.

Initially, it's not much different from a regular traditional massage. Skilled hands massage and caress with the familiar touch of massage oil. Despite the familiar kneading, it's still not quite like a traditional massage. The whole body gets involved, especially certain selected parts that receive extra attention. The well-balanced mixture of caresses and light spanking soon ignites the tingling in her groin, and Susanne realizes she's experiencing the same symptoms as the woman before her. It's simply impossible to lie still; each new touch sends an electric shock through her body, focusing on one particular spot. She moans softly and requests a more hands-on treatment, but Pelle remains unmoved. Undoubtedly, he enjoys prolonging the process that will eventually lead to a liberating climax.

Several curious onlookers gather around the massage table, and a man in the growing crowd around Susanne tries to assist. However, Pelle immediately makes it clear who is in charge. He, and no one else, will deliver the final push that sets the avalanche in motion. After a few agonizing minutes, Susanne finally fulfills her burning desire. Pelle uses a soft brush that barely touches her swollen, blood-filled sex as the tool that pushes her over the edge.

The intense orgasm takes completely over her body, for a brief moment, she seems transported to another world. Even Joakim, who is accustomed to her orgasms, becomes momentarily concerned. She lies motionless with her eyes closed, and it's only when Joakim embraces her, she returns to reality. Pelle releases the cuffs and helps her off the table, and despite the prolonged torment he caused, he receives a heartfelt hug as thanks.

Back in the bar, Susanne recovers, but neither she nor Joakim have the energy to continue, even though it's just past midnight. The taxi quickly takes them to the hotel and the eagerly awaited bed. After the shower, they fall asleep like children, but Susanne soon wakes up with anxiety in her chest. She shakes Joakim awake.

"Wasn't it in the film room that I received the massage? Do you think I was filmed while I was lying there? Could it be?"

Joakim, barely awake, tries to process what Susanne is saying and reassures her, "No, you don't need to worry. I'm sure you weren't filmed. I understand that you didn't have any awareness, but I'm absolutely certain that no one filmed you."

"How can you know that? There could have been a hidden camera," Susanne says with desperation in her voice.

"The fact that it's called the film room is probably because there's a large TV there. I imagine they show porn movies on regular club nights, nothing unusual about that. Try to sleep now; you've probably forgotten about it by tomorrow morning."

"I really hope you're right. I just felt a terrible anxiety. Hold me tight, maybe I can fall back asleep."

With Joakim's comforting arm around her, Susanne eventually falls asleep. At breakfast, she looks at the situation more soberly and agrees that it was just her paranoia playing tricks on her. However, they both agree that it was a delightful and rewarding evening. Especially considering the Norrkoping couple who openly shared their experiences from the French naturist metropolis. The main topic on the way home is, therefore, not where they will vacation next year.

It's solely about how and when they will make their way to the pleasure garden, whose existence they weren't even aware of less than twenty-four hours ago. But there is still a long way to go until their next vacation ... autumn, winter, and spring must pass before they can fulfill their French dreams.

A failed sexual encounter

It is said that time flies when you're having fun, and it clearly holds true. The late summer passed unusually quickly. Just the short distance to and from the mailbox confirms that autumn has arrived. The yellow birch leaves swirling in the northern wind are a clear indication that summer is over for this time.

The day's mail mostly consisted of uninteresting advertising leaflets and bills. The exception was a glossy brochure from Silja Line, offering a nearly free cruise to Helsinki. The possibility of a mini-vacation, a break from the autumn monotony, appeals to both of them. They just need to find a suitable weekend. After some juggling, the practical arrangements are sorted out, and they can look forward to the cruise two weeks later. The next day, Joakim surfs on the website of their home club; Couples in Hearts and stops where members can post ads and messages.

"Susanne, maybe we should post an ad on the club website about our Finland cruise?"

"Why not? It's not unlikely that some other members will be on the same cruise."

"Okay, I'll write a few lines, hopefully we get an answer."

A couple of days later, they receive a response. A couple from Uppsala has booked the same cruise.

"Susanne, we've received a response about the cruise! It's a couple our age, Karola and Kalle. They will be on the same departure and suggest meeting for a drink to see if there's chemistry."

"That's great, write back that we'd love to meet them."

"They also want our mobile number. Should we give it to them?"

"Hmm, I'm not sure. It feels a bit uncertain. Maybe we can get a prepaid SIM card that we can use for these situations, so we can still remain anonymous."

"Good idea, I'll fix that tomorrow and text the number to Karola and Kalle.

Finally, it's time for the Finland cruise. They park close to the ferry terminal and join the seemingly endless line of passengers waiting to board the ship. Bored, they entertain themselves by guessing if there might be any couples who could be their date for the evening. After wild speculations, they narrow down their assumptions to two options.

"We can't make a call here in the queue. We'll have to wait until we get to the cabin."

"Well, I'm a bit curious, but most likely it's neither of the couples we guessed on," Joakim replies.

As soon as they are in the cabin, Joakim makes the call, and a lively voice answers at the other end. "Hello, this is Kalle. Who am I speaking to?"

Joakim introduces himself, and they agree to meet at the entrance of the bar thirty minutes later. It becomes a frantic activity; shower, change of clothes and makeup take time but before half an hour has passed, they leave the cabin. The couple who meets them at the entrance looks suspiciously familiar. In joyful surprise, they realize that Kalle and Karola were actually one of the couples they guessed on during boarding. They find a corner table and order their drinks. Karola and Kalle are sociable and easy going, and soon another surprise emerges. It's a small world sometimes; both have roots in the city of Vasteras. Kalle and Joakim even went to the same school with the same teacher … but despite this, they don't recognize each other.

After finishing their drinks, they decide to continue the evening in the restaurant. Food and wine arrive, and they talk about everything from their upbringing in Vasteras to their future paths in life. There is a pleasant and easy-going atmosphere at the table, but everyone seems to have forgotten or at least temporarily set aside the real reason for the meeting. Eventually, midnight approaches, and Susanne glances at the clock, realizing with horror that the original purpose of the meeting is slipping away.

In an attempt to break the pleasant but, in her eyes, overly social interaction. Susanne suggests that all four moves to the cabin to share a bottle of wine. Karola and Kalle immediately agree. The sparsely furnished cabin has only two single beds, so they sit in pairs on either side of the small table. With wine in their glasses, the pleasant conversation continues, but the clock stubbornly ticks on without anyone taking the slightest initiative. Susanne thinks frantically, and she can see the same thoughts in in Joakim's eyes. How on earth are we going to get things started? I hope they are more experienced and know the trick ...

Susanne discreetly observes their new friends, she has no doubts that they share the same hope. Despite this, the initiative continues to be absent. Everyone waits, not a caress, not even a small kiss. The bottle is empty, and the clock has long since passed midnight. Karola stretches and yawns loudly. "Oh, I'm starting to feel sleepy. I think it's time for us to break up."

Kalle agrees and adds that they would love to meet Susanne and Joakim again. "Maybe we can meet next time we're at the club in Stockholm."

"Absolutely, that would be great," Joakim responds, and Susanne agrees. "We ourselves are at the club quite often, but it would be fine if you gave us a heads up a week in advance."

There are plenty of hugs and kisses before they part ways, but everyone is uncertain and tired, so the evening ends without any attempt at intimacy. When the cabin door closes, the hugging continues in private, soon transitioning to what should have happened much earlier. They make passionate love, but suddenly Susanne pauses in the middle of the act.

"Joakim, we have their number. Call and ask if they want to come back, say it's an 'emergency.' They're probably as horny as we are, maybe something can happen after all."

"Can I call now? It's almost two o'clock. Okay, I'll call. It would be fun if we could make something happen. I'd love to feel Karola a bit closer, and you seemed to like Kalle. We can sleep tomorrow."

Joakim dials the number, and after a few signals, he hears Kalle's voice loud and clear: Hello, you've reached Kalle. Leave a message, and I'll call you back ...

"Well, it looks like it'll be just you and me tonight, but that's not bad. You know I love to fuck you, baby."

"I'm in," says Susanne with a seductive expression ...

At breakfast they meet Karola and Kalle again, everyone has a good laugh at yesterday's pitiful attempt, and Joakims late cry for help. In despite of the outcome, they realize that the attraction didn't fade, the desire is still there. All four promise to do better next time they meet. The discussion soon turns to what went wrong despite everyone wanting the same thing. How do you actually get things started? They agree that they should have started as individual couples, then the hot desire for sure had taken care of the rest. Although the meeting with Karola and Kalle didn't end as they had hoped, they are still happy with the weekend. New friends are not found every day ...

The initial euphoria of discovering the new, hidden world had slightly diminished. Club visits and sex was pushed aside by an endless stream of must-dos. After a couple of weeks, however, the abstinence from club life becomes clear, both agree that it is high time to knock on the now familiar grey door again. The first step is visiting the club's website, especially the upcoming party's section. The Halloween party with a buffet a few weeks later sounds like an event to their liking.

Susanne points out that it could be nice to hide behind some extra makeup and a wild witch wig. "It's like a costume party. I've always enjoyed themed parties; people usually become happy and relaxed."

"Sure, costume parties can be fun, but how will it be here? You won't know who you're fucking." Joakim chuckles.

"That's part of the excitement, isn't it? I highly doubt you would mind fucking a sexy witch just because you don't recognize her?"

"Not at all, eight hundred kroner per couple for both entrance and food are quite okay."

Susanne rummages through her handbag, searching for her calendar. She eventually finds it and lights up with a satisfied smile. "We have nothing planned that weekend. Let's announce our interest."

"Let's do it right away. Maybe we should also look for an online store for costumes and stuff like that." Joakim fell silent for a second and continued with a big smile. "And maybe a new broomstick for you?"

"Yeah, yeah, we'll see what we can find," Susanne replies without commenting on Joakim's poor attempt to be fun.

After sending the party registration and ordering costumes, they continue browsing their private calendar. With a tinge of disappointment, they discover that the coming weekends are filled with unnecessary birthdays and other social obligations. They resignedly acknowledge that the weeks leading up to Halloween will be a period of abstinence, not necessarily free from sex, just without the exciting sex life they had quickly fallen in love with.

Halloween Party with Aftermath

October was as usual rainy and dreary, but all the social commitments at least made the weeks pass quickly, and suddenly Halloween was around the corner. They book the same hotel as their first visit to the club, but with a significant difference; the anxiety and uncertainty are gone. However, it's not only the feelings of worry that have disappeared; the pleasant late summer weather has also vanished in the chilly autumn wind. The low-pressure system that has settled over Stockholm and its surroundings continued relentlessly, offering rain-laden clouds spiced with the occasional autumn storm. At the moment, though, the gloomy weather feels less important with a Halloween party just a few days away.

In the early afternoon they checked into the hotel and after some wine and relaxing in the hotel sauna, they began the transformation process into ghoulish Halloween characters. However, the second step, involving the makeup, is not as easy. It took a considerable amount of time to apply the heavy layers of makeup, predominantly in black and grey tones. Even Joakim gets his fair share and eventually ends up looking more like a chimney sweep than a frightening Dracula.

They laugh heartily at their new looks, which would probably scare both children and adults. For once, the weather is cooperative; the persistent rain has stopped, so they walk the short distance to the club. Almost there, they encounter a group of witches and other dubious characters. One of the witches asks if they are heading to the Halloween party.

"Yes, we are. It's just a couple of hundred meters left," Joakim replies.

"That's great. Then show us the way," the witch says, adjusting her wig.

The group of witches and specters, all seemingly in their mid-twenties to thirties join them for the final stretch to the club. Joakim quietly asks Susanne if she doesn't think the gang that follow them are a little bit too young for the club?

Sussane nods. "Yeah, I thought the same. All seems to be around twenty-five, way too young for the club in my opinion."

The lively and tense young people led by Susanne and Joakim arrive at the familiar grey door. Susanne rings the bell, and they are welcomed by a Halloween witch with wild red hair and bare breasts. The recently chatty young people become very quiet and hesitantly step into the room. However, they calm down slightly when they see all the witch hats and wigs, but just for a short while. The calm quickly turns to new doubts when they realize that many costumes reveal more skin than they hide. The younger witch who led the group regained her composure and asks where they have ended up.

The busty counterpart at the door pointed to the black-clad crowd behind her. "Isn't it obvious... this is the fun part of hell" Smiling she continued, "or more accurately; club; couple in Hearts. You seem a bit lost, are you pre-registered?"

The young witch stared back wide-eyed. "What club?"

When the youngsters finally realized that they have accidentally ended up at a swinger's club, general amusement breaks out. The younger witch stifles a shy laugh, and apologizes. Soon, the bewildered group is on their way out, giggling as they continue toward their original destination.

Susanne and Joakim laugh heartily at the incident but feel confident that they themselves have arrived at the right place. They quickly handle the formalities and immerse themselves in the crowd of witches and specters. Black is undoubtedly the colour of the evening. The difference from a regular club night is that practically everything is black, but fortunately, the atmosphere is brighter.

"Damn, all these sexy witches are making me horny! Why are we turned on by witches? It's a bit twisted," Joakim laughs.

Susanne nods. "Many of the witches are indeed attractive, but personally, I prefer a virile and charming Dracula!"

After some mingling, Joakim looks a bit resigned. "Don't you think this is starting to resemble a regular party too much? Everyone just chit-chatting, kissing, and hugging, nothing really happening."

"I'm not sure," Susanne replies. "Haven't you noticed that completely different body parts receive all the kisses and hugs here? Be patient; things will probably pick up after we eat."

"I hope so; come on, they've started serving food."

They find a couple of available seats next to a cheerful group dressed in black. Everyone is curious about their tablemates, so there are many new names to remember, though only first names, which makes it a bit easier. The atmosphere around the table is lively, and the lively discussions mostly revolve around sex, as expected. However, the conviviality doesn't last long. As soon as everyone is full and satisfied, one couple after another disappears to satisfy a different kind of hunger.

"Come on," Joakim says. "We can't sit here all evening, even though it's nice. We're here to have fun, right?"

Susanne doesn't need any convincing; they follow the flow into the playrooms, where the sounds of activities can be heard from afar.

"Joakim, do you notice the difference? What action! It must be the *masquerade effect* that makes people let loose a little extra."

"Yes, there's definitely a difference. Much more action than on a regular night, but with a little luck, I think we can find a spot for ourselves."

Good fortune favours them, and they find a place between two couples who are clearly fully occupied with satisfying each other, without any helping hands. All three couples focus on their partners, but it's impossible to avoid physical contact completely. The more or less unintentional contact between the sweaty, vibrating bodies enhances the pleasure beyond the ordinary.

Afterwards, Susanne looking loving and happy. "What a ride! I think the couples on our sides felt the same; it certainly seemed like it,".

"Yes, it was fantastic to have you all to myself. I love you. We can have amazing sex, especially when we're alone," Joakim adds with a mischievous smile.

"Absolutely, it was really great, but I'm so thirsty. Shall we sit down at the bar for a while? I'll go to the restroom, sparkling water for me."

With the help of the water, coffee, and some Halloween candy, they soon regain their energy and rejoin the happy and horny crowd. They stop by the *gyn room*, which is unfortunately occupied but they linger for a while as passive spectators. The examination itself appears to be closed. The woman sits back comfortably and receives the treatment, which is suspiciously similar to regular sex. They discreetly enjoy the pleasant show for a while before continuing their trek. It is clear that there are more guests than a normal Saturday, but after the initial excitement subsides, most people seem to move between the playrooms. The corridors are so narrow that they have to squeeze through, but even the close physical contacts do not lead to sex.

"Well," Joakim remarks disappointedly, "we might as well sit down and have a glass of wine, nothing is happening here."

"Not much", Susane replies. "It started off well, but now it seems like everyone is just wandering around and looking. If it doesn't get better, I think we should go back to the hotel and have our own orgy. If they had allowed single guys, I'm sure there would have been more action. I would have appreciated it, at least," Susanne responds with a playful smile.

"What?" Joakim replies with feigned surprise. "You're probably right, but single guys are not allowed. Girls in companion with a couple is okay, but how many times have we seen that?"

"Well, just a few occasions, but I totally agree. Single girls are also needed."

On their way to the cafeteria, they are stopped by a couple of their own age with a cheerful greeting. "Hey there, where are you heading?"

They stop, and the woman curiously fingers the small leather whip hanging from Susanne's hip. "It matches your outfit, where did you get it?"

"It's actually brand new; we found it in a sex shop downtown."

Both seemed friendly and sociable, the conversation soon turned to the club and its pros and cons. Suddenly Susanne stiffens; she clearly feels that the caressing hand that slipped under her dress does not belong to any of the men. Even before Susanne decided how she would handle the concrete invitation, the woman suggests that they go on in a playroom. Susanne glances at Joakim, who nods. She takes his hand firmly and then decisively leads the way to the mirror room. The room is nearly empty, only another couple at the far end. Susanne sinks onto the mattress and soon finds the woman and the man on each side of her. So, what happens now? Is it a partner swap or ...

The answer doesn't wait; the woman immediately wraps her arms around Susanne in a sensuous embrace that cannot be misunderstood. Joakim seeks eye contact with Susanne, and he receives an immediate, sensual smile in return. Harshly, he realizes that the partner swap he had hoped for is going to be one-sided. The girls clearly manage just fine on their own. Susanne eagerly awaits what comes next. Before she knows it, her body is covered in demanding caresses. Only aware of what is happening in her immediate proximity, she soon finds herself engulfed in a cloud of pleasure that she neither wants nor can escape from. Joakim is now convinced that it wasn't him who attracted the couple's attention, but what does it matter? He leans back and enjoys watching Susanne's expressive face as she succumbs to the impending climax. Tenderly, almost lovingly, he sees how the woman caresses and hugs her while the orgasmic spasms slowly subside. Back in reality, Susanne gazes into a pair of dark, friendly eyes.

"Welcome back, my name is Anita and this is Kenneth. I apologize if I was a bit brusque." She shrugged innocently; "Your sensual gaze totally carried me away."

"Oh, don't worry, I'll gladly accept your apology, but I have to agree with you; you were quite determined. I understand it wasn't the first time you took care of a woman. Anyway, I can don't complain about the treatment. My name is Susanne and this is Joakim."

"Nice to meet you," says Joakim and gave Anita a hug. "I didn't participate much, but being a spectator wasn't bad either. I really enjoyed watching, and it was clear you both had a great moment."

"Shall we take a break in the cafeteria?" Kenneth suggests.

"Sure, I feel a little weak after ... well, whatever you did to me," Susanne replies with a satisfied smile.

Anita and Kenneth were no exception; they are sociable and easy to talk to, like many other swingers. In the cafeteria, they have a pleasant conversation, and it doesn't take long before all four agree that the chemistry was unusually good.

Before parting, Anita asks if they have any plans for New Year's Eve. "It would be great if you could come to our place. It'll only be the four of us, we can do the food together, and I don't think we need to spend the evening in front of the TV." Anita suggested with and inviting smile.

Joakim looks questioningly at Susanne. "I don't think we've made any plans yet."

"I haven't even thought that far ahead, but it sounds nice. We can get in touch during the upcoming week," Susanne replies.

"Yes, please do. It would be lovely to take care of you guys." Anita gave Joakim a blink. "And of course, I mean you too, Joakim. We live in Saltsjöbaden, and you can stay overnight if you want."

They thank them for the invitation and promise to get in touch soon. Anita and Kenneth leave for a waiting taxi. Joakim realizes that another fantastic evening is coming to an end, but he's still a bit frustrated, as he hasn't found a Halloween witch for himself yet. There are no objections from Susanne, so they venture back into the play-rooms for another round. Fortunately, most of the people who previously wandered through the corridors have finally found their way to the mattresses in the play-rooms.

They take a place between two couples and let their hands slip toward the nearest pair. A heavily made-up woman with a tousled dark purple wig and a bloody Dracula with hair in a poisonous green colour. The invitation is accepted and soon they are tumbling around on the mattress. Joakim gives Susanne a happy look that is met by an equally satisfied smile before they forget each other for a while. After returning to their respective partners, they catch their breath and begin preparer for the walk back to the hotel. The conversation naturally revolves around their new acquaintances and what happened in the mirror room. Susanne happily concludes that it was a most successful evening and Joakim nods in agreement. Even the New Year's invitation does not lead to a longer discussion; they simply cannot find a reason to decline it.

The few weeks leading up to Christmas fly by, and a week before the holiday season, the dream of a white Christmas is ignited. The outer suburbs of Stockholm are covered in a thin layer of glistening white snow, but as usual, it doesn't last very long. After just a couple of days, the snow changes colour to a gloomy greyish-black hue. Christmas and the days between Christmas and New Year, which are usually a welcome break from the winter darkness, feel more like a transition period this time, leading up to the New Year's weekend. They had since long accepted Anita and Kenneth's invitation. They are supposed to be there by eleven o'clock, unusually early for a New Year's dinner but necessary, according to Kenneth. The time was needed for a surprise to the girls ...

A Different New Year's Eve Celebration

Christmas and the remaining days of the year ended quickly. On the morning of the very last day of the year, Susanne is busy packing for the short trip to Anita and Kenneth. Eventually there is a neat row of bags in the hall. Joakim looks at the considerable amount of luggage with a skeptical expression.

Susanne, will we stay a week or what? At least it looks like that. How on earth did you manage to fill up three large suitcases?"

"Well, it's bedding and the clothes for the evening, and then an extra bag with some changes of clothes for me, plus my favourite toys. Beside of that I had a hard time deciding which shoes to bring, but now I have a few options to choose from."

"I understand, but do we really need a huge suitcase just for shoes?"

"The shoes, and especially the boots, take up space, but it's nothing to worry about. We probably won't have to carry the bags very far."

"Probably not, I'm just a little surprised at how much stuff we've managed to gather for just an overnight stay."

Susanne is eager to get going. She can't help but show her impatience for the surprise Kenneth has promised.

"Yes, I'm so curious about what Kenneth has planned. Do you have any idea what it could be?"

"Not a clue, but a not-too-wild guess is that it has to do with sex."

"Probably. Otherwise, I'll be both surprised and disappointed."

New Year's traffic runs surprisingly smoothly and they arrive at Anita and Kenneth in good time. They barely have time to step inside before they receive a glass of champagne. However, Kenneth has to settle for a modest sum in his glass. Anita raises a toast.

"Great to have you here. When I asked you at the club, I didn't really believe in the idea myself, but I'm so glad you accepted the invitation."
Susanne nods happily. "We're glad you asked. We felt we had such a good connection, so we wanted to see you again. But Kenneth … what kind of surprise have you come up with? I'm really curious."

"Well, here's what I thought. Joakim and I will take care of the food for the evening, but before we do that, we'll drop you ladies off in the city. We'll leave you at the central station, and then you'll find out what mission I've come up with."

"Joakim raises an eyebrow. "Mission? What kind of mission?"

"No, I wasn't going to tell you anything more, not right now, anyway."

Susanne looks questioningly at Anita. "Do you know anything of this?"

"No, he hasn't said anything other than that he has arranged something fun for us. I have no idea what it is, but I can guarantee it has to do with sex." She turned to Kenneth. "I suppose I'm right, honey?" Anita asked with a suggestive smile.

"Maybe," Kenneth smiles. "I've written down a few suggestions that I hope you'll like, and as I said, you'll find out more when we drop you off."

"Okay, I suppose we can't escape," says Susanne with an expectant expression.

"I don't think so," sighs Anita. "But let's finish this drink so that we can get going."

When they arrive at the central station, Kenneth takes out an envelope. "Here you go … well, what should I call it? Some tips on how to pass the next few hours."

"Oh, the famous instructions. What have you cooked up?" Anita sighs and accepts the envelope with a skeptical smile.

"Well, it's a bit like a genie in a bottle, but instead of three wishes, there are three missions, and I think you've already understood that they have to do with sex. Actually, only one of the missions is described in detail. As for the other two, you must use your dirty imagination, but I can't imagine it will be a big problem for you. But for heaven's sake, don't take it too seriously. The idea is just to have fun and maybe get a little horny along the way."

"What? Don't you think we already are?" Susanne responds, and Anita giggles in agreement.

"Oh, I know that already. The idea is simply to add some spice. Just see it as a suggestion, a fun thing. You'll do whatever you want anyway. Now, for heaven's sake, we don't have time to stand around here. We have to go home and start with the food. Let me know when you want to be picked up."

Anita suggests that they start at the pub in the central station. "We don't really know each other at all, so starting with a beer or a glass of wine might be a good start."

"Absolutely," agrees Susanne. "Let's have a drink and see what he's come up with. You have the envelope, right?"

"Oh, yes, I have it in my bag. I wonder what that horny man has come up with."
With a beer on the table, they open the envelope and find three handwritten pages adorned with a few naughty pictures. They giggle like teenage girls as Anita quietly begins to read. "I think my dear husband is a bit disturbed," Anita manages to say between fits of laughter.

However, Susanne defends Kenneth. "I think it's cute, well, maybe cute isn't the right word, but it's definitely a fun initiative. I'm so curious, what is he writing?"

Anita takes a sip, clears her throat, and reads in a low voice. "When you come home, we guys will make sure you're pampered a little bit extra. We will make an effort to treat you to a delicious dinner and an erotic New Year's Eve with you girls at the center. The idea behind the missions is for you to get to know each other and hopefully get aroused, while also tickling Joakim's and my imagination."

Susanne interrupts, "If the guys want to be tickled, we might as well make sure they are, right?"

"Sure, I like crazy antics," Anita responds.

"Yeah, me too, but what does he want us to start with?"

"He wants us to send some 'naughty' pictures with our phones."

Susanne looks thoughtfully at Anita. "Hmm, naughty pictures... where on earth can we take those, there are people everywhere?"

"Good question, maybe we can go into the ladies' restroom together," Anita suggests. "Otherwise, I'm not sure how we can pull it off."

"The restroom will do. A picture of us peeing cross-legged might get their imagination going, what do you think about that?"

"Great idea, that should be kinky enough to tickle their imagination. Plus, we'll probably need a restroom after the beer."

"Okay, that's the first mission. What else has he come up with?"

Anita quietly reads through the second mission. "Well, he wants more pictures. He suggests that we discreetly expose ourselves in the crowd, hmm, that might be difficult."

"Yeah, I'm not sure I'm keen on showing my breasts, or anything else in public. I think we should skip that mission, or what do you say?"

"Absolutely, exposing ourselves is not my thing."

"And the third mission, is it just as crazy?"

"Nah, but it's still a bit twisted," Anita giggles. "We're supposed to go into a restroom and take off all our clothes, everything! Then when we meet the guys, we're supposed to be completely naked under the coats, not even wearing panties." Anita smiles when reading the last sentence. "He finishes by saying we'll have the backseat all to ourselves on the way home."

Susanne smiles back, "he's a bit twisted indeed ... I think I know what he expects to see in the rearview mirror."

"Oh, yeah, I know exactly how that rascal thinks. Luckily, the rear windows are really dark, in case we're in that mood." Anita says, shaking her head silently.

"We'll see what happens," giggles Susanne.

They finish their beer while chatting about family and work. The feeling from the club is amplified; they can easily relax and be natural with each other. With anticipation, they look forward to Kenneth's crazy missions and the upcoming evening.

After a while, the beer takes its toll, and they join the queue outside the ladies' restroom. After a few minutes, a toilet becomes available, and amid giggles and laughter, they start the first mission. The restroom is small, but after they get rid of some clothes, Susanne eventually sits astride Anita with the phone set to camera mode. Peeing after a large beer is not difficult, but taking pictures that show something interesting at the same time is not that easy.

"Now I've taken five shots, hope one of them turned out well," Susanne says and gives Anita a quick kiss.

"At least one should be okay. Now we just need to put our clothes back on and get out of here. Judging by the knocks, there are more people in need of the restroom, the queue is probably even longer than when we arrived."

After a quick freshening up, two giggling girls leave the restroom, and as Anita feared, the queue was now considerably longer than before. They don't receive any cheerful smiles directly, and the glances clearly indicate that they weren't as quiet as they thought. They hurry away, still giggling, leaving the women in the queue behind. However, the next item on the agenda has nothing to do with Kenneth's missions. They interrupt their antics with some shopping, but before that, they send the pictures from the restroom.

"Kenneth, your phone beeped. Check if it's something from the girls, I'm really curious."

"Yes, it is! Come, we have to see if they managed to get something interesting."

The first picture is dark, making it difficult to distinguish any details. What stands out most clearly is a pair of legs and then something in the middle with dark, indistinct contours.

"That blurry thing in the middle is probably what we really wanted to see," Joakim says with a hint of disappointment in his voice.

The other pictures aren't much better, but the accompanying message at least gives them a tingling sensation: Hey, we're in the restroom, peeing cross-legged. The pictures are a bit dark, hope you can see something. Kisses wherever you like.

They laugh to the crazy idea of peeing cross-legged. Even though the pictures didn't show much, it started up their imagination - How did they do, who was on top, and so on ...

Joakim is brought back to reality by Kenneth's voice. "We need to fix the soup before we pick up the girls, let's hurry up a bit."

Anita and Susanne had a more relaxed time, they finished their shopping round with a late lunch.

"Susanne, I'm not really up for taking daring photos in the crowd, didn't we agree to skip that?"

"Yeah, let's go straight to the third suggestion as soon as we finish eating. Doesn't that sound good?"

"That's absolutely fine," Anita replies and continues,

"Even though we'll have the coats to hide under, it will still be a bit thrilling."

"Yeah, but let's do it! Call the horndogs and tell them they can pick us up in half an hour."

The restaurant's accessible restroom is much more spacious than the one at the station. Dresses and underwear quickly come off, and the bags from their shopping spree come in handy for temporarily storing the surplus clothing.

"This is really crazy," Susanne says giggling as she puts on the coat. "Are we really supposed to go like this? I feel truly naked."

"Yes, it does feel insane. Imagine if we slip and break a leg, the paramedics would have a good laugh," Anita giggles.

"Despite being a crazy idea, it does tickle between the legs a bit, does it feel the same for you?"

"For sure, it's a tingling feeling down there," Anita confirms.

Susanne checks the time. "But hey, we need to go now. Was it at the parking garage by Hötorget we were supposed to meet them?"

"Yes, that's what we said. We'll call again when we're close. I don't want to stand and wait in this minimal attire; they better make sure to be there on time."

A quick hug, and they leave security in the restroom. No suspicious looks meet them this time, it's just two happy women in leather boots and long coats... After a short walk to Hötorget, they meet the guys. Once in the backseat of the warm car, they let their coats slide apart to show that they have completed the third mission. All four have a good laugh at Kenneth's crazy ideas and a happy party goes home.

Susanne gives Anita a long hug. "Thank you for a nice afternoon, it has been both fun and interesting getting to know you better."

"Ditto, it's been great, and it could be even more fun. Lean into me and relax."

Susanne takes off her coat and sinks into the seat. She closes her eyes and willingly accepts Anita's sensual caresses. Absorbed in lust and excitement, the girls forget that only the dark side windows protect them from the outside world.

Joakim, who is grateful that he does not have the role of driver, is torn between the desire to participate in what is happening in the back seat and the pleasure of just being an observer. For Kenneth it is worse. Despite the temptation to let his eyes linger in the rearview mirror, he manages to focus quite well on what is happening in the direction of travel.

When the traffic suddenly stops over a pedestrian crossing, Joakim can't help but smile. Stressed pedestrians rush around the car in all directions, but no one seems to notice what's happening just an arm's length away. Turning his gaze back to the back seat, he breaks into an even bigger smile. The girls haven't even noticed that the car has stopped. They are too busy at the moment to care about such mundane things as a bit of chaos in the afternoon traffic. The sensual play in the back seat continues until the car finally stops at Anita and Kenneth's house.

"What? Are we home already?" Anita exclaims in surprise.

"Yes, indeed," says Kenneth, unable to suppress a laugh. "Time flies when you're having fun, doesn't it?"

"Yes, it went quickly," agrees a misty-eyed Susanne. "It was an unusually pleasant ride and we got home without any mishaps, at least not that I noticed. You must have kept your eyes on the road more than in the rear-view mirror."

"Well, I did sneak a few glances, but not as many as some others. Joakim must have gone stiff in the neck from staring."

"Oh yeah, I noticed." replies Susanne with a challenging smile. "I guess it tickled your fancy, but that's what you wanted, wasn't it?"

"It definitely tickled my fancy," said Kenneth, continuing in a hasty tone. "But we have some things to do in the kitchen, close your coats and at least, try to look decent. The neighbours would pass out if they saw you like that."

While the guys take care of the last details for the dinner, the girls shower and make themselves beautiful for the evening. Finally, they all relax with a pre-dinner drink before sitting down at the table. The intensely green pea soup with a splash of brandy turned out perfect, and the compliments continued when the bloody sirloin was served.

The girls' experiences during the afternoon are naturally a hot topic of conversation. The boys are curious and eagerly absorb all the details. But it's not just the afternoon's adventures that are discussed; more general joys and sorrows are openly shared, and their friendship deepens further. It will be a long and pleasant gathering, interrupted only by the stroke of midnight. After the new year has been properly toasted, the evening ends with easy play on the sofa ... and Joakim and Kenneth also get to join in on a corner.

After a long, pleasant breakfast Susanne and Joakim pack their bags into the car. The next meeting is already planned; Anita and Kenneth will come over in four weeks. Once in the car, the conversation inevitably turns to the experiences of the previous day.

"They are wonderful, I really like both," says Susanne.

"It's only the second time we've met, but it already feels like we've known them much longer than that."

"Apparently it's easier and faster to form relationships in this world, compared to the more official one. I had a great time with Anita, we became very close."

"It's clear... you came very close," replies Joakim with a smile. "Kenneth and I also connected well, but not quite the way Anita and you did. It's a bit of a shame there wasn't a partner swap, but I have to say it was a super nice New Year's Eve."

"Yes, it would have been exciting. I wouldn't have minded having sex with Kenneth and I understand that you would have wanted to be with Anita," says Susanne.

"Absolutely, but she seems more interested in same-sex experiences?" asks Joakim.

"Sure...but I'm surprised that I've accepted her initiative so easily. Could it be like Eva said, women are more open to same-sex relationships? But now, especially after yesterday I've realized I like having sex with both men and women. Anyway, maybe the partner change will happen when we get to know each other better?"

"We'll see when they get to us. It's sure to be a nice night anyway." answers Joakim.

After a moment of silence Susanne starts: "Joakim, have you ever thought about how quickly and easily we've gotten into this? It's apparently extremely easy to get used to having sex with others. Not that I have any reservations, but it's clear that we find it hard to do without it," Susanne says.

"Well, it's definitely addictive, that's for sure. It would be difficult to quit, wouldn't it?" Joakim agrees.

Susanne nods in agreement. "Absolutely, in any case I have no plans to even try. But on the other hand, we should probably take it easy sometimes. It can't be healthy to have new sex partners every weekend."

"Of course not. If it comes to that, let's hope one of us realizes that we're treading on thin ice," Joakim suggests.

"We should be careful not to end up in some kind of sex addiction," Susanne responds thoughtfully but brightens up and adds, "Which, after all, must be preferable to other drugs ..."

"Sex addiction feels distant, but we have another problem. How do we explain to Ida and Jens that we've made new friends?" Joakim asks.

"Hmm, good question... Maybe we can just say that we met them on a cruise to Åland and they invited us over for coffee. What do you think about that?"

"Well, that will have to do." Susanne sighs resignedly.

The rest of the winter goes by, and the darkness and cold are noticeably easier to endure than in previous winters. They meet Anita and Kenneth several times, and they now feel like truly close friends. Between the meetings with Anita and Kenneth, they also visit clubs in

Stockholm and Norrköping. They make new contacts, most of whom are pleasant and social, but the deeper sense of connection is missing. On the other hand, their sense of belonging with Anita and Kenneth grows. And they have the same feeling for Karola and Kalle, the couple from the Finland cruise.

At one occasion, they invite a couple they've only had online contact with, and it doesn't turn out well. The woman was pleasant and outgoing, but her husband was reluctant to participate in the play. He also does not excel in social situations; he seems content to be a bystander to the threesome that could have become a successful foursome. Without the boring husband and his dry comments, it would probably have been a completely successful evening. But there is nothing bad that does not have something good with it, the lesson is clear and unambiguous. Never invite people without meeting them first, preferably in a neutral location.

Spring and summer are approaching and the holidays feel more urgent than ever. Memories of the couple's Norrköping vivid description of the naturist metropolis have only strengthened, and the countdown has begun. The only thing that might disturb their dreams is the element of naturism, which will be a whole new experience.

Joakim's thoughts mainly revolve around the part of his body that sometimes tends to have a mind of its own. How on earth is that going to be? Will I walk around with a hard-on all the time? Hopefully not, it's probably the same as with fragrances. No matter how nice they are, eventually you stop noticing them.

Susanne also has her own thoughts and concerns: Mingling with a bunch of other naked people, how will it be, will everyone be naked, didn't Karin say that you only have to be naked on the beach? But what about Joakim? Will he just wander around looking at all the younger and fresher girls? Well, in that case, I'll just enjoy the well-built guys. No ... I shouldn't jump to conclusions. We usually get along well, even in situations like this.

The French Paradise

After a long wait, it's finally time to pack their bags and let Ryan Air take them to Girona, Spain. The last two weeks in August will be enjoyed in the French naturist metropolis; Cap d'Agde. Rental car and apartment are booked, everything is sorted and ready for a hopefully delightful and eventful couple of weeks.

After a punctual landing in Girona, they pick up the rental car and let the GPS guide them to their long-awaited destination. The queues in the final stretch are indeed taxing, but eventually they can park outside the entrance to the naturist area. However, the wait is not over yet. The reception at the main entrance is packed with people eagerly waiting to access the area and their accommodations. Entering the area is not as simple as walking through, as all guests must be duly registered and scrutinized. However, it's not Saint Peter deciding who is allowed to pass through the gate of the naturist paradise. The responsibility has been delegated to a few leisurely ladies who surprisingly speak decent English. Finally, the wait is over, their booking is in order, and after a few more questions, they receive a confirming nod and a "bienvenue sur Cap d'Agde."

They have passed through the eye of the needle; the gate to paradise is wide open. Excited and curious, they pass through the open gate, finally there... Now they just need to find the apartment. According to the map they were given at reception, it is in an area aptly named Heliopolis - The Sun city. Despite its size, the large circular complex, consisting of several hundred apartments only a small part of the naturist metropolis. The entire fenced area is significantly larger and at first glance looks like any resort, but with a distinct difference. Most of the *citizens* are as expected, only dressed in their birthday suits. Despite this, the first impression is unexpectedly mundane. Some are heading home with bags full of groceries, others are carrying umbrellas and sunbeds on their way to the beach. The mundane scene doesn't last long though, the shock of the nudity hits them full force. Suddenly it becomes impossible to focus on the directions and in a confused state they circle an extra lap of a roundabout before finally finding the car park and their home for the next two weeks.

Joakim smiles. "Isn't it amazing, there are naked people everywhere. I know we're in the naturists' Mecca, but it still feels a bit unreal."

"Yes, but strangely enough, it just looks natural. Actually, you would stand out more if you were wearing clothes," Susanne giggles.

Joakim hesitates before getting out of the car. "Hmm, should we undress before we go up to the apartment?"

"No, I will keep my clothes on while carrying our belongings to the flat. Later, when we go out to explore the area, clothes won't be a sustainable option."

The apartment, or rather *the hole in the wall*, is a textbook example of compact living. A not-too-wide double bed, a kitchenette, a toilet, and a shower are squeezed into about twenty square meters. The space also includes a wardrobe and kitchen furniture, the free floor area is far from a dance floor. Despite the minimal space, it feels good; at least it's clean and tidy. The best part, however, is the small balcony with a lovely view of the sea. Once all their belongings are neatly stowed in the compressed space, a long-awaited shower awaits. After that, there is no turning back; now they have to face the challenge and venture out among all the free-spirited naturists.

"Joakim, we should start stocking up the fridge. I think there are all kinds of stores within the area, even groceries."

Shouldn't we start with the beach? I really want to feel the water. The couple we met in Norrköping said it could be quite cold, depending on the winds and currents."

"Sure, let's start with the beach."

Joakim smiled. "Are you ready, now you can have no problem choosing clothes!"

"Don't say that. I was thinking of wearing a thin scarf around my waist, and I actually have two to choose from."

"Not a bad idea actually. It feels like we want something more than just sandals. I think I'll pull a beach towel over my shoulder," replies Joakim, looking satisfied.

Out in the crowd, they see that many, like themselves, are wearing a scarf or a towel. While it doesn't hide much, it at least gives the illusion of clothing.

"Joakim, it actually feels quite okay to walk around like this. I didn't really expect that."
"I think you get used to it quickly; after all, this is how we are born. Cornelis was probably right."

"The troubadour ... you're thinking of the lyrics to his nudist polka?"

Susanne nodded. "

"If I remember correctly a line goes like: Being naked clears my mind. That's absolutely liberating to be naked among other naked people. Good old Cornelis, he was probably righter than he realized ... or even more likely, he knew what he was talking about."

The walk down to the so-called family beach only took a few minutes. Families with children and retirees dominated this part of the beach, everyone was naked except for a few teenagers. They quickly concluded that most couples without children had found their way to the more interesting part of the beach

Susanne kicked off her sandals and took a few steps into the water.

"Wow, they were right," she exclaims. "It feels more like the lakes at home than the Mediterranean. Lucky, we didn't come here just to sunbathe and swim ..."

Joakim stepped out in the water. "Oh, it's not too bad. I you lie in the sun and get warm it will be quite ok. Anyway, I guess you'll get hot for reasons other than the sun too ..."

"You're probably right. When we get to our actual destination, it probably won't be as peaceful as here", replies Susanne.

"Probably not, but now we're going to look for a shop so we can get something to eat and drink. But first, I need a cold beer, just sit down and relax. There are probably plenty of shops and bars in the mall we went past."

They stopped at café 1664, named after the French beer. When the finished the drinks, they continued to explored the mall. Most of the stores had focuses on clothing and shoes with an emphasis on sex and erotica, the category was clearly overrepresented. Many items in these stores were seductive, ranging from beautiful erotic lace garments to tough leather outfits, not to mention the supply of sexy shoes and boots.

"Susanne, you know I love seeing you in something sexy,' and there's so much of these things here. Just look at those dresses, not to mention that leather corset. "

"Calm down, I'll probably shop until you're speechless, but not today. First, I want to explore the other stores a bit. I suspect there are more than what we've seen so far."

"Sure, but I noticed something else. There wasn't a single fitting room in any of the stores we went into... but I guess it's not necessary in a place like this."

"No, I guess you just try things on where you stand. After all, everyone is naked , so convenient." Susanne smiles contentedly. On their way back they found a well-stocked grocery, just a few steps from café 1664.

Back in the apartment, exhausted from the journey they take a nap. The debut in Cap's swinger world can wait. Later, after some thoughts they dress up and get ready to venture out into the warm August night. Outside the door, they are greeted by a strange, alluring scent. Impossible to define, perhaps a mix of plants and the steaming pots of the restaurants? With the pleasant aroma in their nostrils, they make their way towards Port Nature, the pulsating center of the area.

For the evening, their primary focus is a good dinner. However, the wide selection of restaurants doesn't make it easy to choose, ranging from simple pizzerias to gourmet establishments. After some searching, they choose a restaurant strategically placed along the main promenade.

"Joakim, I want a table where we can see people walking by. I could probably stay here all evening just enjoying everyone dressed up for the night."

"Absolutely, we must have a table where we can enjoy all the eye candy. It's almost unbelievable."

The restaurant proves to be an excellent choice for anyone curious about Cap's spectacular dress code. Many had clearly put a lot of effort into standing out from the crowd. After a year as swingers, they were convinced they had seen it all when it came to sexy and obscure outfits, but that was about to change. Very soon they became aware that it was just an illusion, the variety of extreme outfits seemed endless. It was obvious that the clothing choices at the Swedish clubs were nowhere near the never-ending stream of spectacular-dressed people and indeed, some completely naked ...

In addition to bars and restaurants, they passed several clubs. Finally, they stopped outside Club Glamour. The queue outside gave a clear indication that it was a good starting point. The music pouring out of the open doors along with all the dressed-up people made them rethink their plans. For a brief moment they considered joining the snaking queue but finally decided, despite the temptation, to stick with their original plan. The club premiere had to wait until the next evening.

The sun is already high when they wake up, the heat is noticeable in the small room. Outside, it is still calm and quiet, even though it's nearly nine o'clock. During a long and enjoyable breakfast on the small balcony, they slowly come to life along with the other inhabitants of paradise.

After breakfast, they pack their bags for a full day at the beach. A baguette, a bottle of rosé, some water, and a couple of beers. Food and drinks are accompanied by sunscreen, towels, books, sun umbrellas, and more ...

"This feels more like camping rather than a day at the beach," Joakim sighs in frustration.

"Come on, stop complaining. We're just on our way to swinger's beach. For God's sake, we're on vacation, relax!"

On the way they pass the sheltered, well-mannered part of Cap's extensive beach. There is already a flurry of activity there. Teenagers and parents play beach tennis, Frisbees fly over their heads while the younger kids build sand castles or just play happily on the beach. Susanne notes with pleasure that it is not only swingers who appreciate Cap's beautiful beaches. They enjoy the sun and feel surprisingly comfortable, despite the lack of clothing. There is heavy traffic in both directions along the shoreline, everyone doing their best to avoid the hot sand and instead let the waves cool their feet. With the sights set on the long-awaited beach they leave behind the playful families and naturists with their bushy sexes.

For a brief moment, the distance between the beach umbrellas widens, only to shrink considerably as they arrive at the infamous beach. The space between couples is sparser than they expected, it's not difficult to find a place. Through their sunglasses, they discreetly enjoy the surroundings and the relaxed atmosphere. Many of the couples lie close together or strategically rest a hand on an interesting body part. Others purposefully caress their partners, but no one seems to go all the way, at least not at the moment.

The image that the couple from Norrköping conveyed turned out correct, at least so far. Most of the nearby pairs appear to be around their own age, but there is a wide range. From twenty-five and up to those who have long since passed retirement age. Consequently, there is also considerable variation in physical appearance, ranging from young fit gods and goddesses to those who have completely neglected their bodies

The beachgoers also display a diverse range of more or less imaginative ways to enhance and decorate their bodies. Many women adorn their private parts with rings and jewellery made of precious metals. Although there is a clear majority for the female gender, there are also a few men who embellish their genitals with shiny, glistening rings. However, the hot trend for the girls is something entirely different; a metal anal plug with a sparkling stone that glimmers seductively when this part of body is turned toward the sun. But as with all spectacular fashion trends; far from everyone has embraced this daring style. Something much more common is a considerably older method of body adornment ... tattoos. A significant number of women, and probably about an equal number of men, bear tattoos with every conceivable and inconceivable motif. The most tasteful tattoos are often found on the women, particularly popular is the tribal patterns on the lower part of the back. Many have also honoured their most intimate body parts with beautiful artworks.

Joakim tries to relax, but the hot sun combined with all the women unabashedly displaying their well-groomed genitals and other enticing attributes constantly distracts him. Even Susanne is influenced by the highly erotic atmosphere and eventually lets her fingers wrap around Joakim's sun-warmed erection. The lighthearted atmosphere surrounding them is overwhelming, but the merciless sun becomes too much, and the cooling waves feel increasingly enticing.

Isn't it time for a swim? It's getting unbearably hot," Susanne suggests.

"Hmm, I don't know if I want to go right now. I'm still a bit hard."

"A bit ..." Susanne laughs. "That's a good hard-on."

"Yeah, yeah," Joakim grins, "If I close my eyes for two minutes it will go back."

"No one here cares if you're hard as stone or not. They might think you have a giant cock. Come on now!"

"Alright, but then I have to be quick into the water."

"Yes, show that you're not a wimp."

With quick steps and a swaying erection, Joakim finds his way between towels and parasols. Once in the water, he discovers that it is extremely shallow and also cold... He ignores the chilly water temperature and rushes out the protective waves. Relieved, he notices that no one seems to mind his predicament; there are only happy faces and thumbs up. Once again, he receives confirmation that this beach is not like any other.

The rest of the afternoon passes without them or the couples around them causing any major infractions of the local regulations. As the hours pass, they relax and realize that the choice of holiday destination feels just right. They enjoy the peace, which is only occasionally interrupted by muffled orgasmic screams. However, the sun and heat are a challenge, but with the help of the sun protection and the small parasol, they manage to stay until the shadows grow larger.

Suddenly something happens, and the previously calm beach undergoes a drastic change. Crowds form in several places, large circles of curious onlookers quickly appear, along with a marked increase in the noise level. Susanne and Joakim get curious and walk towards the nearest circle. They join an elderly French gentleman who explains in broken English that the beach police have finally given up for the day, and now there's no holding back the emotions. A massive wave of pent-up desire is unleashed. Several couples are already engaging in sexual activities with their partner, some even inviting interested onlookers.

Even those who try to be discreet have to endure enthusiastic cheers from other couples and lone, masturbating men. Some of the lone males have fully mastered the art of wandering around and in their search for interesting jerks of objects. Usually, these men spend a significant part of the day with one hand on their more or less erect genital. With surprising speed, they position themselves where something is happening and are often a clear indicator that something interesting is about to take place.

Wide-eyed, they peer into the circles and let themselves be gratefully entertained by the spectacular spectacle. They stop at a large circle where a Spanish couple is putting on a playful show. The woman straddles the standing man and holds his neck with her hands. With a firm grip on the woman's buttocks, he thrusts frantically. Every now and then he releases his grip, stretches his arms to the sky, claps his hands and roars, "Look, no hands!"

The performance is rewarded with whistles and applause, which obviously adds to their excitement. Even the couple's small poodle observes the playfulness of their owners and adds to the atmosphere with persistent barking. The whole scene continues as the woman gets down on all fours and is spanked playfully, in sync with the applause of the audience. The crazy show ends with the man ejaculating over her with exaggerated cries of pleasure.

"Joakim, this is absolutely crazy, the talk of reality surpassing fiction couldn't be truer."

"It's hard to believe what we're seeing, but maybe we should tear ourselves away. It would be nice to take it easy before we go out for the evening."

They pack up and head home, but nature makes its presence known. Joakim realizes that he is in desperate need of a toilet, but such luxury does not exist on the beach. Peeing in the ocean is perfectly fine, an approach that has been fully embraced by naturists and swingers alike. However, the vast sea is not suitable for all kind of needs. But the solution is not far away. On the way home, they sneak into the naturist campsite next to the beach. With only one day's experience of naturist life, Joakim looks for a men's toilet but soon realizes that such a thing does not exist. Men and women, why should there be any difference in a naturist area? The showers lack doors, but luckily you can close the toilet door.

Joakim sighs gratefully. Thank goodness that the toilets at least have doors. I have no problem having sex in front of an audience, but to shit in public, no way ... you have to draw a line somewhere.

Back in the apartment, Joakim takes out the camera and takes a few pictures of the sea. Suddenly, Susanne realizes that they don't have, and won't have, many vacation photos suitable for the family album.

"Joakim, we need some vacation pictures to show the kids and our regular friends. We'll have to take a few pictures with our swimsuits on, then it will look like we're on a regular vacation."

"Haha, good idea. I'll set up the camera, and we can take some pictures in here and on the balcony."

They found their swimsuits at the bottom of the bag and posed in front of the camera with happy faces. It's hard to hold back the laughter, but eventually they manage to capture the traditional, innocent vacation photos. After the photo session, they enjoy a salad and get some sleep before the impending club visit.

New experiences in Cap d'Agde

The nudity is over, at least for now. Susanne puts on her favourite dress, a tight black leather dress and stay-ups. Underwear and a bra feel unnecessary. Joakim chooses a pair of light-coloured pants and a tight black T-shirt. After a last touch they are finally ready to go. The first destination of the evening is Pizzeria Flora in Port Am-bonne, according Karin and Magnus; the best pizza you can find in Cap. The restaurant is only a five-minute walk from their apartment, but Susanne's high heels and the open evening shops slow them down. Instead of a few minutes, it takes half an hour ...

The pizzeria is definitely not one of the most exclusive restaurants with its long tables and wooden benches. Despite its simple appearance and spartan interior, it is one of the more popular eateries in Cap. The stern "Madam Flora," or Bébé, as she is more commonly known, is a sight to behold. She runs the restaurant with a firm hand and keeps her staff tight reins. Even the guests have to endure Bébé's often curt and brusque responses, but she is also quick to reciprocate a smile.

After a ten-minute wait in the que, with the scent of hot stone ovens in their nostrils Susanne and Joakim sit down on the long benches. They are surprised to discover that the benches, which initially give a cheap impression, have their advantages. It facilitates interaction with the people next to them, at least in cases where a common language is found. The next surprise is the menu, which is even translated into Swedish and various other languages. They realize the uniqueness of this situation as they are in a country where all sort of information is usually only available in French. The service also seems to work well as the rosé wine arrives quickly, and the food not long after. After enjoying a pizza that undoubtedly lives up to its reputation, they venture out into the bustling crowd. There is still an hour until midnight, and the clubs have just opened. There is plenty of time to familiarize yourself with one of the numerous bars. The endless stream of people leads them past the strip bar Melrose, which seems to be a hot spot. Despite it still being early in the evening, it's already packed with people. The techno-inspired music creates a compact sound barrier that effectively hinders any conversation at a normal level. They squeeze into the crowd, and the first thing they notice is the loud waitstaff and their brusque manner. Swiftly moving and carrying trays high, they navigate through the dense crowd of onlookers. A rude sample of French profanity quickly teaches them not to get in the way of these stressed balancing artists.

Despite their skills, the notorious waitstaff is not the reason for the bar's popularity; the main attraction is the pole dancing, and the guests themselves provide most of the performances. Many women, and even a few men, seize the opportunity to showcase their abilities or, in some cases, the lack of talent and self-criticism. The girls who climb onto the bar counters for the dance pole often focus more on emphasizing the absence of underwear than on displaying advanced dance. Cheers and applause often depend more on the amount of exposed skin than on the dancing performance. Many feel inspired, but Susanne chooses to stay on the floor despite, Joakim's encouragement for a dance number

The bar visit is a nice interlude, but after a while they leave the chaos of Melrose to go to Glamour, the club that caught their interest the night before. They join the compact crowd that squirms like an amorphous amoeba outside the bar, the stream of leather, latex and bare skin slowly leading them towards the bars and shops of Port Nature. But time is ticking slowly, it's still too early to head to the club. They settle down at a bar by the sea, have a glass of wine and continue to enjoy the evening flaneurs passing by.

 After a visit to the toilet, Joakim returns with a broad grin. "Susanne, what a place, it's crazy. When I came out of the toilet there was a girl kneeling behind the bar giving the bartender a blowjob. You could just see it coming out of the toilet; the people at the bar didn't notice. I know I nagging a little, but this is just crazy."

 "Well, what can you say? It's insane... liberatingly insane," agrees Susanne.

They continue their wandering and suddenly Joakim whispers, "Check out the group over there on the right, the ones in leather. Wouldn't surprise me if they're Germans."

Susanne can only agree. "Wow, those clothes are amazing!"

"Do you see, they have the fair-haired girl on a leash?"

"Yeah, but she doesn't seem very submissive the way she talks and walks. By the way, she's having a really nice ass."

"Absolutely, I wonder where they're going... Anyway, cheers to our upcoming club visit, it's going to be really exciting," says Joakim, raising his glass.
Susanne answers the toast and waving to the waiter.
"Sure, but finish your drink and let's go, there should be a few people at the club by now."

The night is still young, at least by French standards. It will probably be an hour or two before there will be the same kind of queue they saw yesterday. They pay the fee, forty euros which also includes two drinks. The bar and dance floor look like any other trendy venue; they had expected something completely different. The only hint that it's not just a regular disco are some cages and platforms for pole dancing. The techno music pushes on to attract more visitors, but so far only a few couples have dared to step onto the shiny dance floor. One of the couples drops the dance and instead offers a hot live show

The techno music pushes on to attract more visitors, but so far only a couple have dared to step onto the shiny dance floor. the dance soon turns into a hot live show. They truly seem to enjoy being the center of attention.

The staff behind the bar chat and enjoy the calm before the storm. So far, they don't have to put in much effort to take care of the few guests who have found their way to the club. Joakim counts seven couples in addition to the couple on the dance floor. Some hang out at the bar, others on the sofas. Not much happens, they decide to explore the playrooms in the basement before more guests arrive.

They explore the downstairs imaginative playrooms. It's maze with dim lighting, and as usually; colors in red and black. Time and again, the long, winding corridors put your sense of direction to the test. To begin with, it seems they are the only ones who ventured there. But on the way back they stumble upon an English couple who are evidently as lost as them self. Also, the Englishmen turns out to be newcomers at Cap's club scene. All four of them laugh at their foolishness of going to a club before one o'clock. After a few more minutes of conversation, they agree not to waste any more time on talking. The large fake-leather bed literally screaming for the evening's first adventure. However, the English, or maybe the French routine is a bit different from what they are used to. Here, partner swapping happens straight at square one ...

After the inspiring experience with the English couple, they continue their wandering through Glamour's winding corridors. Immediately, they notice that more expectant guests have been lured down to the sofas and mattresses of the playrooms. Besides the fact that the club is much larger than the Swedish clubs, the procedure is the same. When they find an appealing couple, they simply position themselves next to them and try some light caresses on a neutral body part. In most cases, the invitation is received positively and reciprocated generously. It becomes an intense night, around four o'clock, the guests start to trickle away. Susanne and Joakim also stumble home, tired but satisfied with their club premiere.

The following days, they visit other clubs and manage to squeeze in a few more visits to Glamour before their departure. The late-night club visits, however, take a toll on their sleep habits, with each new day shifting their circadian rhythm a few degrees. During the last few days, they arrive at the beach only after lunch, but in return, they stay longer and enjoy the free shows generously offered.

The days pass quickly, and their temporary visit to paradise draws to a close. On the penultimate day, they have lunch again at the restaurant near the part of the beach they have come to highly appreciate. They order their favourite dish, mussels cooked in garlic. The mussels from the nearby farms taste divine, also the locale rosé wine tastes fine. After finishing their meal, they silently enjoy the view below, but the silence doesn't last long. Susanne takes a deep breath and speaks with a determined tone.

"I refuse to go! I have to put this beautiful image in my mind, all naked people and the sparkling sea in the background, it's priceless. Can't we order more rosé and just enjoy the moment?" I will need that when the winter-darkness threatening to suffocate one.

"Not a problem for me, we have no time constraints," Joakim replies, waving to the waiter.

In a state of bliss, Susanne raises her arm and says, "Look, really look. Have you ever thought about how damn beautiful naked people are? It doesn't really have anything to do with sex. From here, I think everyone looks like small works of art, regardless of age and body shape."

"It's true that resting your eyes on a naked body is delightful. I can definitely appreciate the sight of a well-trained male physique, but you women have something magical about you. Your breasts, lips, everything is so perfect, both to see and touch."

Susanne gives Joakim a dreamy grin. "You are absolutely right; the female body is lovely in so many ways ... but a naked man is equally beautiful, but maybe in a different way."

"Yes, indeed, but perhaps the most wonderful thing is seeing a jumble of naked men and women openly enjoying each other without inhibitions. I know you agree with me," Joakim says, receiving a subtle nod as confirmation.

They enjoy the wine in the shade of the parasol and let the image of the sparkling sea with all the living works of art in the foreground etch itself into their minds. It's an image to recall and draw strength from when the darkness of winter feels heavy. Eventually, the second carafe runs dry, and in high spirits, they leave the restaurant to return to the beach. Joakim goes ahead and waits for Susanne, who lingers. After a couple of minutes, he turns back. He finds her engaged in a cheerful conversation with a charming couple, a few years younger than themselves. Joakim smiles in recognition when he realizes that they are, in fact, the Germans in their tough leather outfits. He greets them with a broad smile and thinks to himself. How wrong can you be? They're definitely not Germans, they're pure Stockholm natives ...

"Joakim, this is Maja and Max. Have a seat, we're not in a hurry."

It turns out that the couple are well acquainted with Cap and its surroundings; it's far from their first visit here. Max orders another pitcher of rosé wine, and after an hour or so of intense conversation about life in general and Cap in particular, they agree to meet in the evening. Maja suggests meeting at Le Look bar, neighbour to the noisy, Melrose. According to Maja, the bar primarily serves as a meeting place for gay guys and trans individuals but has also become a popular spot for heterosexual couples. She adds that Le Look is the complete opposite of Melrose; here, you can have a conversation without having to shout yourself hoarse.

They arrive slightly early for the meeting and have a glass of white wine while they wait. Le Look has a simple interior and doesn't stand out in any particular way, except for the interesting mix of guests. There is a significant predominance of men and some remarkably tall women. Despite encountering a clientele, they are not quite accustomed to, they soon find themselves agreeing with Maja's praise. The staff is friendly and polite, unlike the rough-edged waiters at Melrose. Moreover, it's actually possible to have a conversation at a reasonably moderate volume. Maja and Max eventually show up. The conversation continues in an interesting mix of life experiences., both within and outside the swinging world. A couple of hours later, they part ways after exchanging email addresses and phone numbers.

Before bidding farewell, Max suddenly brightens up. "A friend of ours is hosting a pool party in September. It would be great if you could join us."

Both Susanne and Joakim look surprised at Max. "Can you invite us to your friend's party, just like that?" Susanne asks, wondering.

"Oh, yes," Max laughs. "We know each other very well, so it's completely fine. They are like you, beginners in the game and around your age. Besides, I'm sure you'll fit in well among the other guests."

"Sure, that sounds really nice," Susanne replies. "But maybe it would be better if your friend sends us an invitation themselves. You can give them our email address, right?"

They walk slowly home in the warm August night, somewhat thoughtful about the upcoming pool party. "We'll see if we receive an invitation," Joakim says with a hint of scepticism in his voice.

"We'll find out, but if they do reach out, I think we should definitely accept, don't you think?"

"It's always nice to make new acquaintances, especially in this world. At least it has been like that so far."

"Absolutely," Susanne responds. "But now I think we should go home and get some rest, so we'll be fresh tomorrow."

However, their last evening at Club Glamour doesn't turn out as successful as they had hoped, but it serves as a valuable reminder that the best sex they have is still between the two of them. Swinging is just a spice, albeit a tasty one. The next day, they leave Cap d'Agde with a touch of melancholy. Most of their experience has been overwhelmingly positive, with exciting encounters, new friendships, and, last but not least, the discovery of the life-affirming naturist lifestyle. They return home with a firm belief that they haven't seen the last of the naturist paradise. At least Max's invitation to the party gives them something to look forward to in the near future. However, they are far from convinced that they will actually receive an invitation.

A new stage of the journey

Back home the daily routine hits them with full force, but with a certain difference. Typically, there is a club visit or a meetup to look forward to. Max's promised party invitation is still after two weeks conspicuous by its absence. The doubts grow with each passing day, but their surprise is even greater when it turns out that they after all were not forgotten. Happy they read the email, signed by Helena and Svante. The invitation appears fairly innocent, enticing them with good food and pleasant company. The closing remark, mentioning that more information about other activities will follow later, hints that it's a party to their liking. The date of the party, two weeks later, fits well into their schedule. They immediately accept the invitation and a few days later, the promised information and directions arrive in their mailbox. The day of the party eventually arrives, and after the obligatory preparations of choosing clothes and shoes, they are finally on their way. Joakim focuses on the driving direction, while Susanne ponders how the evening will unfold.

"Do you think there are different rules at private parties, compared to the clubs?"

"Well, it's probably more social compared to the clubs, but hopefully, we won't just be socializing around the dining table. I'm really looking forward to seeing Maja and Max again."

"Absolutely, and there might be others we recognize, maybe some we've met in Solna or Norrköping."

The address leads them to a newly built villa in a quiet area. The address leads them to a newly built villa in a quiet area, at the door they are greeted with a warm smile.

Hello, you must be Susanne and Joakim. It's great you could come. I'm Svante. You can either have a glass of wine with me and Helena in the kitchen, or you can jump straight into the hot tub."

They start by stowing their bags in the room where they will eventually sleep and then peek into the kitchen. Despite Helena rushing back and forth between pots and serving dishes, they receive a hug and the same warm smile from her as they just did from Svante. After a brief stop in the kitchen, they let the cheerful chatter guide them to the hot tub. There, they are met with a row of unfamiliar but friendly faces. The only ones they recognize in the lively gathering are Maja and Max.
After a very informal introduction, they shower and then squeeze down among the others in the hot tub. The positive vibes are evident; no one seems to be bothered by the decrease in private space, rather the opposite.

Susanne finds a spot between a man and a woman and immediately feels at ease. Joakim, who ended up between two guys, feels a bit uncomfortable. Not the ideal position, but the relaxed atmosphere soon makes him overlook the physical contact with the men. In some strange way, they skip the usual steps when it comes to new acquaintances. No one asks the common question, *So, what do you do for a living?*

Without clothes, occupation and social status feel less important, while personality and social competence rank much higher. Joakim can't help but smile as he looks at Susanne; she has truly changed. Less than two years ago, she was reluctant to enter a sex shop. Now, she sits naked in a hot tub with a group of unknown swingers, actively participating in the general discussion. She seems totally engrossed in a serious conversation about male and female sexuality, with a man who rests his hand on her breast.

Joakim soon has other things to think about. He freezes when he suddenly feels a hand move towards his groin. Is it really the guy next to him touching him, but he quickly calms down when he sees it's a woman's hand. But one of the guys next to him has noticed his reaction, and he soon feels another hand on his thigh, a rougher one ... To his relief, the hand quickly let's go, Lukas laughingly apologizes for scaring him.

"Oh no, it wasn't that bad. You can come across worse things," Joakim smiles strained.

The pleasant moment in the hot tub is coming to an end; it's time to get ready for dinner. As usual, the women require a little more time than the men who gather in the kitchen and have a beer and socialize in general. Eventually, everyone can sit at the table. Apart from the guests' daring clothing choices and the women's slightly heavier make-up, it's like any other party. Everyone chats away, and the topics of conversation are surprisingly universal. Helena and Svante's efforts with the food do not go unnoticed and many return time and again to the tasty buffet. Both guests and hosts seem to be in good spirits and discussions of varying seriousness follow each other. No one seems to have any intention of leaving the pleasant company around the table.

After a while Joakim begins to feel restless; he strongly believes that the social part of the party should have ended much earlier. The upstairs area with its imaginative sex toys and inviting mattresses, glimpsed earlier, is still waiting for its first visitors. He becomes more and more doubtful whether the evening will offer any sexual activities at all.

However, salvation is not far away. A slim woman with dark hair apparently has the same thoughts. She can't contain herself and disappears under the table to sample what her table companions, male as female have to offer. The guests around them make a few appreciative comments but soon go back to finding solutions to world problems and everyday matters. However, the woman's initiative soon rubs off on some of the other guests; a man diagonally across from Joakim starts purposefully caressing his table partner. Soon the woman shakes in an intense orgasm, that for a moment brings all conversation to a halt. However, most guests quickly resume to the exquisite dessert not even being distracted by the couple on the couch who fuck like rabbits. Finally, a pants-less man speaks up and declares with an authoritative voice that it's high time to explore the facilities upstairs. Some continue conversing without raising an eyebrow, but most take the suggestion seriously and make their way upstairs.

After another half hour, all the guests are finally gathered on the upper floor, and the real party can begin. Susanne and Joakim stay behind and curiously observe a swing made of wide leather pieces and heavy chains. Its function is not immediately apparent, but Svante soon arrives and explains the swing's ingenuity. With a little help, Susanne manoeuvres herself onto the wide central piece of the swing and realizes that the seemingly illogical construction is actually well thought out. The clever swing spreads her legs and opens up her private parts, like an orchid enticing its prey. Evidently, the tactic works in this world as well; several guests immediately gather around the flower, that so clearly demands attention. With anticipation, she closes her eyes and surrenders to the hands that explore her exposed petals. In vain she tries to count the hands that caress and grab her but is eventually forced to open her eyes. Somewhat shocked, she notes that there are two women and two men, but she is quickly reassured when she sees that Joakim is by her side.

The small circle around the swing takes care of her in an extraordinarily lustful way. She closes her eyes once more and embraces the pleasure offered to her with an open mind. Through half-closed eyes, she sees Joakim sitting on the floor. At the moment he is satisfying the dark-haired woman who has her face buried between Susanne's legs. The familiar feeling in the underbelly quickly intensifies, and after just a minute, a wave of pleasure washes over her. For a moment the surroundings cease to exist, it's only when a blood-filled shaft gently presses against her lips she opens her eyes. The scent and touch of the smooth glans awaken immediately the desire. Susanne eagerly closes her lips around the hard member, and without letting go of her newfound toy, she manages to issue a determined request to Joakim. "Fuck me, give me cock, please... right now!"

Her obsession rubs off on Joakim, who wastes no time in fulfilling her request but can barely penetrate her before losing control. His only thought is to unite with Susanne in her orgasmic heaven as quickly as possible. when she wakes up from the orgasm bubble, she gratefully accepts the support from the leather-swing supporting her currently heavy body. Joakim, in turn, has sunk to his knees and rests his head against her genitals, where the aftershocks still pleasantly tickle. Suddenly, she sees a smiling man in front of her, waving invitingly with a condom. Susanne, still not fully recovered from the intense orgasm, raises her hand and shakes her head in refusal.

The condom man understands the hint and responds cheerfully, "Maybe I can come again later?"

With Joakim's help, she wriggles out of the swing and makes her way to the nearest sofa on unsteady legs.

"Please, can you fetch me some water? I feel completely drained after that orgasm."

"After that orgasm ..." Joakim smiles. "You had at least three, maybe four orgasms while you were on the swing."

"What? Are you serious! I didn't sit there for that long?"

"Nah, just about half an hour or so."

"What? It felt more like ten minutes! Anyway, I had a really good time, regardless."

The evening continues as it began, with bathing, food and sex. In the playroom's sofa, Susanne and Joakim indulge in the remaining treats from the buffet together with another couple while witnessing a frenzy of oral sex on the mattress in front of them. Two women and a man engage in a playful threesome. Alternatingly, the women help each other reach the heights of orgasm before returning to the object of their desires between them. The man, increasingly becoming a toy in the women's hands, eventually succeeds in giving them the hotly desired reward.

Despite the entertainment they enjoyed during the late-night meal, they don't have the energy to get properly aroused, and gives finally up for the night. Once they have settled into their sleeping arrangement, they make a valiant attempt to summarize the evening and put names to all the cozy, horny people they met. However, they don't succeed very well, and after a short while, they fall into a deep sleep. Not even the final lustful cries echoing in the night disturb them in their dreams.

After a few hours of sleep, they wake up to the sound of chatter and happy voices coming from the kitchen. The hosts and several guests are already up. The aroma of freshly brewed coffee wafting upstairs creates a pleasant and homely feeling. Anyhow, the pleasant impressions from the kitchen have to stand back for the memories of the previous night's events. Foreplay is unnecessary; it becomes an intense and passionate quickie. Ten minutes later, they sit with their coffee cups in hand, joining the others who managed to get up. Everyone seems satisfied and happy, openly discussing the events of the previous day with laughter and excitement. It turns into a long and enjoyable breakfast in a cozy atmosphere. Once breakfast is over, it's time to restore the house to a presentable condition, stowing away sex swing and other necessary toys. After completing their cleaning efforts, Susanne, Joakim, and the other guests gather their belongings, which were scattered throughout the house in the heat of passion.

Black panties and stockings are to be found everywhere; the challenge is simply finding the right panties and pairing up matching stockings ...

After exchanging nicknames and email addresses, a minor kiss fest before they finally get in the car.

"Joakim, what a fantastic party! We met so many nice, wonderful people, especially Helena and Svante."

"Yeah, this is hard to beat. Everyone was so positive and super horny. I had great sex with Gun and with… um, what was her name? She with long hair and silicone breasts who slept in the same room as us."

You mean Sabina?"

"That's right, but how about you? Are you happy with the evening?"

"Absolutely. I just have to say it feels safe when you keep track of things. Without that I wouldn't be able to relax like I did on the swing."

Yes, you really enjoyed yourself." Joakim said with a big smile.

It was so wonderful with all the hands caressing me, and it felt really good to be licked by Gun. She knew what she was doing," says Susanne, adding: "Actually, everything was great, but the best was when you took me into the swing, you were wild."

"I got incredibly horny when Gun took care of you. I really get turned on when you're with another girl."

Well, it seems that Eva was right, she from the dark-room on Couples in hearts. Most girls in this world are actually more or less bisexual. Apparently, I fit that template too, although I prefer men, but what about you? I noticed Lukas went a little handy with you when we were in the bath."

Joakim shrugged his shoulders. "Well, it was mostly a joke, or he just wanted to test me. Sure, I was surprised when I felt his hand on my thigh, but I'm not homophobic, it was okay."

"Anyway, it was a great party, not to mention all the delicious food they served."

"The food was great, but I think we sat at the table a little too long. At one point I doubted there would be any sex at all. By the way, who did you have at the table, was it Gunnar?"

Susanne, replied with a smile. "Yes, he was very nice and sociable. He told us, among other things, about an organization called Pleasure Chamber, it sounded really interesting. They have a website that we'll check out when we get home."

"Absolutely, I sat between Helena and Gun. We had some interesting discussions, mostly about sex but also about more mundane things. Helena mentioned that there's probably going to be a party later this fall, and I really hope we get invited to that is the case. A lot of people in this group seem to have been in the lifestyle for a long time, I hope they didn't think we were too much of a novice."

"I don't think so. I think we fit in very well. I would actually be surprised if we didn't get an invitation," Susanne answers confidently.

Back in the peace of their own home, they sit down at the computer and easily find the Lust chamber's website. The photo dominating the homepage is spectacular; a naked woman hanging in a huge spider web, but that's as far as they can go since they are not members. They can only read the information on the homepage, which is enough to keep their curiosity alive.

"That sounds good," Susanne says cheerfully. "Don't you think?"

"Absolutely, we should contact the webmaster."

They apply for membership and are accepted. Neither of them has any idea how much this membership will expand and enhance their network within the swinging community.

The following weekend is calm, at least from a sexual perspective. The birthday party at their old friends' house starts off with pleasant mingling, but already there, they notice the difference compared to last weekend's party. Hugs and greetings feel stiff and artificial, overall, the atmosphere is a bit subdued and restrained. The conversations are form Susannes and Joakims perspective very pale and pointless. Everyone is careful not to bring up sex or other sensitive topics.

Susanne discreetly whispers to Joakim, "If we miss out on these kinds of gatherings, I don't have a big problem with it."

"That's great, then we share the same opinion. Hopefully, people will loosen up when they have a bit more alcohol."

"I really hope so, otherwise, we might have to come up with an excuse and head home. At least we've become really good at emergency lies," Susanne replies with a wink.

The atmosphere gradually improves as the evening progresses, but not everyone can handle the abundant amount of wine. The bag-in-box concept, as practical as it is treacherous, unsurprisingly has less pleasant consequences. The topics that were avoided at the beginning have taken off but unfortunately, often with an unnecessarily high volume. A couple of guests end up in a heated political discussion where a fight seems imminent. The poor hostess, who is also the subject for the party, manages in the end to quiet down the overly intoxicated gentlemen, tears welling up in her eyes.

Crude and sex-related jokes that no one dared to make earlier are now heard frequently. The orderly gathering of guests who sat down at the table is no longer as neat as before, the red wine stains mixing with other traces from the dinner table speak for themselves. Susanne glances with ill-concealed disgust at her table neighbour, trying to determine if it's food residue or vomit that are glimpsed in his beard. Finally, and to everyone's relief, the most intoxicated guests start making their way home. The group of guests thins out more and more, and eventually, Susanne and Joakim also head home, somewhat unsteadily.

"I don't understand," complains Joakim, "how the hell did I get so damn drunk? I always had something in my glass, who the hell kept refilling it?"

"You probably got a little help from our attentive hostess, but most of the time, you probably made sure you had something in your glass yourself," Susanne laughs.

Joakim stares blankly ahead, shaking his head in disbelief. "I prefer swinger parties; there you don't get this damn intoxicated. It was a dam luck we had a walking distance back home; a taxi ride would probably have made my stomach turn inside out. Well, we'll see how I feel tomorrow, I'm afraid not much productive will be done."

Susanne just sighs and nods in agreement ...

The Party Continues

The party that Helena and Svante had at their house obviously left them wanting more of that kind. A new party is planned later in the fall, and Joakim's hesitation about being invited turned out to be unfounded. The timing of the party is well chosen, as who doesn't need something to brighten up life when the November darkness does its best to make us feel down and hopeless? The week before the party, Susanne mentions to Ida and Jens that they will be away for the weekend.

"Oh, you're going to another party, have fun," is Jens' only comment.

When it comes to Jens' sister, she doesn't get away so easily. Ida is much more inquisitive than her brother ...

"That sounds nice, where are you going? Do I know anyone there?"

Susanne thinks for a second before answering, "No, you don't, they're friends of Anita and Kenneth."

"Oh? But why were you invited to their friends?"

"Well, I'm not sure, they apparently wanted more guests, so they asked Anita and Kenneth if they had any nice friends."

"A bit daring to invite people you don't know, but it sounds like a fun idea. I hope you will have a good time. I assume you'll be staying over at Anita and Kenneth's as usual? Oops, I'm late. Sara and I are supposed to be at the gym in half an hour."

As soon as Joakim is home, Susanne tells him what she said about the weekend party. "Jens didn't ask anything, but Ida was more curious. I felt compelled to come up with something new. We can't always be at parties at Anita and Kenneth's, so I said we're going to their friends'. Just so you know, it's good if we say the same thing if it comes up. It doesn't feel good to have to lie, but it would be even worse to tell the truth."

"That sounds believable, and it's good to know what to say if they ask. Our hobby is definitely not something they need to know about."

"No, definitely not."

"So, Ida was more curious, isn't typical for girls to be nosy?"

"Well, it's probably a feminine trait. We're usually a bit curious and interested in what's happening around us."

"You don't think she suspects anything?"

Susanne spins around and stares at Joakim. "No, I don't think so. We've been very cautious and discreet. Her questions were probably just driven by healthy curiosity. God, I dare not even think about what would happen if they found out. Ida would surely be shocked."

"Maybe, but I still don't think she would make a big deal out of it. Jens probably wouldn't care much, and after all, Ida isn't that different from her brother."

"I'm not sure..." Susanne says with a hesitant voice but soon brightens up. "Well, well, as long as we continue to be discreet, hopefully we won't have to worry about that. But hey, I've been thinking about something completely different. We don't meet our old friends very often."

"True, but on the other hand, maybe I don't miss all of them equally. I think we still hang out with those closest to us, like before."

"We probably do, but in the end, maybe we'll only socialize with swinger friends if it continues like this," Susanne says with a pensive expression.

"I don't think so. We'll surely keep in touch, at least with some of our old friends."

"Well, we can't completely cut ties just because they're not swingers, and who knows," Susanne continues with a mischievous smile. "Some of them might even share our interest in more open-minded sex?"

"I don't think there's much pointing in that direction, but never say never ..."

After a few more days, the long-awaited bright spot arrives, and suddenly November doesn't seem so dull. The familiar routine takes over, clothes are chosen, bags are packed, and finally, only party makeup remains. Many people are already in place when they arrive, most of them familiar from the first party, but they also discover a few new faces. Especially Kajsa and Henrik arouse their curiosity, both Susanne and Joakim get positive vibes from the newcomers

They don't have time for a long conversation before it's time to head to the hot tub.

In the shower, Susanne whispers, "Kajsa and Henrik seemed nice, didn't you think?"

"Absolutely, they felt genuine and easy. Maybe we can play around a bit, we'll see what happens when the real party starts."

"I'm up for it. But come on, let's jump into the pool now."

The atmosphere in the pool is just as relaxed and cozy as last time. Everyone is chatting and there is playful touching here and there. Susanne starts a discussion about the problem of wearing swimwear on public beaches. However, the discussion is interrupted when two more women squeeze in. The overcrowded pool is now filled to the brim, and the intensified physical contact adds to the charged atmosphere. After just a couple of minutes it becomes a jumble of arms and hands caressing and hugging, making it difficult to determine who is touching whom. The conversation stops completely, and is soon replaced by contented moans. But the orgie is short-lived, Svante who was about to mention that the food is almost ready, stops abruptly. He bluntly declares that he doesn't want any bodily fluids diluting the pool. The message is heeded, and the orgy ends as abruptly as it started. One after another leaves the pool, and heading off to the showers and the anticipated dinner table.

The food is as well prepared and delicious as at the last party. The unpretentious conversation flows in a relaxed atmosphere, interspersed with playful sexual activities. After a while, Svante gets up and calls everyone to move upstairs ... a new sex toy waiting to be inaugurated.

With unadulterated joy, Svante presents his new toy, a Sybian - the Roll Royce of all vibrators. The toy, or rather the machine, is basically an unusually powerful massager built into a curved plastic box that the user sits on. One of the advantages is that you can choose between several interchangeable dildos, depending on personal preferences. Then you just have to sit down, lean back and let the intense vibrations do the work. You can either control it yourself or let a bystander take over the remote control. According to Svante, the device guarantees a quick and powerful orgasm.

Curious comments immediately fill the air, especially from the women, but of course the men also want to see if the machine lives up to Svante's vivid description. Lena is the first to step up, with a satisfied smile she chooses a thick dildo and holds it provocatively in front of her partner.

"Tobbe, this one is almost like yours."

"Thanks for the compliment, but I'll take care of this," Tobbe replies laughing, and quickly picking up the remote control. Deliberately slowly, Lena prepares herself and the dildo with an abundance of lube. Eagerly encouraged by the spectators, she slides down onto the machine and with an expectant smile lets the dildo slowly penetrate her.

"This feels good even without vibrations ..."

"That's good, but now you're going to get vibrations too." A faint hum is heard when Tobbe turns the knob on the remote control.

Lena immediately lights up. "This is something other than my own pathetic toys."

Tobbe continues to play with the remote control, which is directly reflected in Lena's body language. Like a rider in full gallop, she presses her pelvis harder against the vibrating monster who gradually takes control of the situation. Tobbe grins as he turns the power up to maximum.

The hum of the electric motor increases significantly, and the effect is instantaneous. In pure astonishment, Lena widens her eyes and throws her head back with a gurgling sound as the orgasm forcefully grips her. Only with the help of a couple of attentive friends, she manages to stay in the saddle and await the continuation. After another intense orgasm, it's enough. The helpful friends make it clear that it's time for her to pass the reins to the next rider. For a minute, Lena hesitates but then rises on wobbly legs, takes a few steps, and collapses exhausted into the nearby sofa. She hugs Tobbe and teasingly says, "Darling, you certainly fuck like a god, but this devilish machine is definitely a competitor for that title..."

Lena's short but passionate performance has immediate effects. Two couples are deeply engaged in an intense fuck on the adjacent sofa while others satisfy themselves or their partner. The machine continues to hum its song in unison with the rider, this time it's Gun's turn to ride. She too becomes deeply involved in the fight with the machine but is soon forced to capitulate to the tsunami of orgasm that mercilessly washes over her. In the end, most of the women have tried the monster machine, including Susanne. Despite the strong orgasm it gave her, she's not overly impressed, commenting matter-of-factly, "It was a nice ride, but I still prefer the real thing."

After the intense start, most people take a break, relax in the pool or take a bite of the leftovers from the buffet washed down with some wine. With renewed energy Susanne and Joakim return upstairs, they settle down on the sofa in the playroom. Kajsa and Henrik have also returned and stop curiously at the peculiar swing. Kajsa half-heartedly tries to sit in it, but soon gives up on the complicated swing. But help is not far away ...

It's not as complicated as it looks. I tried it the last time we were here. Once you get in place, it's really comfortable. Joakim claims I sat there for half an hour," says Susanne with a shrug and an innocent smile.

Joakim hugs Susanne, "I can definitely testify that she enjoyed it."

Kajsa looks a little doubtful at first, but curiosity takes over. With the help of Susanne and Joakim, she will soon be safely in place.

"Is that okay? Are you comfortable?" asks Susanne.

"It feels good, but I feel a bit exposed with my pussy in the air.

Henrik just smiles and slowly begins to fuck her while tenderly whispering: "Honey, maybe this will make you forget the vulnerability?"

Soon other feelings take over and she gratefully accepts Susanne and Joakim's helpful hands. After taking care of Kajsa together in the best possible way, they help her down from the blessed swing.

"Wow, that was amazing! Thanks for showing me how it worked and, most importantly, for taking such amazing care of me. But shouldn't we take a break? At least I need some coffee, and maybe the rest of you also need a break?"

"Absolutely, coffee sounds good. I think you're as sold on the swing as I was," replies Susanne and gives Kajsa a hug.

"That was great!! She looks at Henrik smiling. "I think we need a swing like that, don't you think?"

"Absolutely my darling, I make one for you."

There is a long break and all four are curious and want to know more about each other. The dialogue is cheerful and positive and Susanne and Joakim's first impressions turn out to be correct. Before they get back upstairs, Kajsa and Henrik receive an invitation to Susanne and Joakim's three weeks later.

Just like at the last party, it's a mix of sex, food and happy laughter. Some focus more on the social aspect after the initial release, while others relentlessly engage in erotic encounters. For Susanne and Joakim, an event like this still has a pleasant veil of novelty over it. They cannot help but be enchanted by the relaxed and warm atmosphere to which most guests generously contribute. Serious discussions on various topics are mixed with light topics. A butt is spanked playfully while others provide themselves with wine and snacks, all in a lovely mix of humour and a good dose of humility.

It's another successful party, and the evening fades quickly. Eventually, even the most persistent give up. One by one they disappear to their sleeping quarters or a waiting taxi.

However, the party is not completely over yet. The cozy communal breakfast remains. Breakfast cereals and sandwiches are enjoyed in the same pleasant and warm atmosphere as last time. Everyday topics mix with humorous anecdotes from previous parties, new connections are solidified, and email addresses are exchanged. After a collective cleanup of sex toys and mattresses, reality starts to set in, and the cars roll homeward. Susanne barely has time to close the door before she heaps praise Svante and Helena once again.

"They're so good at organizing parties. This was just as successful as last time. That big massage machine was fun to try, but the best part was getting to know Kajsa and Henrik. I really hope they can come the weekend we talked about."

"They'll probably come. I think the chemistry was so damn good, and it felt mutual."

"Absolutely. I was also fond of Sandra and Johan. Granted, they are younger and more fit than us, but I still think they liked us. Johan was really turned on by me, at least."

"For sure, he liked you ... even though you almost drowned him with your orgasm, or... maybe because of it?"

"Yes, he actually asked for it, so he only has himself to blame," replies Susanne cheerfully.

"Hope they invite us to that Christmas party. They plan to rent a spa in Uppsala, on Boxing Day. It would be so much fun to meet again, Sandra is such a wonderful woman."

Susanne nods. "It's not just you who is attracted to her, she's lovely.

"So, it seems we have similar tastes in women?"

"Hmm, that's a good question, you know I prefer guys but I'm really attracted to Sandra. She's so… well what can I say, her whole body oozes sexuality. Not least her butt, I'm totally convinced that it's not just guys who want to get inside her panties."

"Hmm, that's a good question, you know I prefer guys but sure, I can definitely be attracted to a girl like Sandra. She's so … well what can I say, her whole body breathes sexuality. Not least her butt, I'm fully convinced that both boys and girls go after her."

"I can only agree, she is delicious."

"Although we might turn on the same type of girls sometimes, I don't think we have exactly the same taste in the matter. For me, it's important that girls are soft and not too demanding. I have an easier time with tough guys. If they get too demanding, I have no problem saying stop."

"It feels good, I mean you can speak up. It's actually you girls who decide in situations like this."

"Yes, but I can imagine that a lot of people who don't know how it works see women in this world as victims, think that we are being taken advantage of."

"They would only know who the real victims are..." Joakim says with a twinkle in his eye.

"Ha, ha, even though we girls usually have the last word, I have a hard time seeing guys as victims."

"No, I can't say I feel like that"

"Got it..." says Susanne and continues. "When we get home, we can start by entering email addresses and nicknames for our new friends. We also mustn't forget to thank Helena and Svante for another successful party."

"It sounds like a decent Sunday job considering that we didn't get that many hours of sleep. If we have a little energy to spare, we might as well rake some leaves, the snow is coming soon," Joakim sighs resignedly.

What shouldn't happen ... happens anyway

The weeks rolled on with an unusually high number of weekdays leading up to the Christmas break, or at least it felt that way. The meeting with Kajsa and Henrik was a welcome ray of light in the autumn darkness. They came on a Saturday in mid-December, and the feeling from their first meeting at Helena and Svante's place was confirmed. It became an evening filled with many good laughs, even during the more intimate moments. The bonds deepened further during the forest walk the following day, and a new meeting at Kajsa and Henrik's place was planned for the end of January. Now there was something to look forward to, even after the long weekends. To their delight, they also received confirmation that the spa appointment on Boxing Day should happen as planned. Both Susanne and Joakim were looking forward to meeting Sandra and Johan.

They celebrated the Christmas Eve together with Jens and his girlfriend. Ida spent the Christmas holidays at her boyfriend's parents' house. The food and other traditional Christmas attributes were quite traditional, but the classic Christmas celebration had still been scratched at the edges. The ham and meatballs now had to coexist with delicious seafood and even the Christmas present hysteria had subsided. Christmas dinner was approaching, but before that, other traditional Christmas activities awaited. This year's mulled wine must be tasted, and a well-known TV classic must not be forgotten. Although the Disney characters have been a faithful tradition since childhood, the well-known clips made everyone smile. After Disney, Christmas presents were handed out, but now days without Santa's help. Then while waiting for the richly filled Christmas buffet, after an hour or so they can sit back on the sofa. There they are treated to another TV classic, this time an old feel-good movie with a predictable happy ending. After the film, the media content shifts from image to sound, and they have the opportunity to enjoy melodic rock music. Slowly they sink deeper and deeper into the sofas while the ham sandwiches are washed down with frothy Christmas beer.

Although it is not particularly late, Susanne's eyelids grew heavier. She excused herself and went to bed. A short while later it was the same with Jen's girlfriend. Joakim and Jens stayed behind, opening another Christmas beer, the rock tones were now replaced by the soothing sounds of The Beatles' "Rubber Soul" LP. Joakim enjoys the pleasant mix of music and relaxed conversation with his son. Everything feels superb, and King Bore himself enhances the Christmas peace with a gentle snowfall. But suddenly, the evening takes an unexpected turn. Without warning, Jens clears his throat and begins stumbling.

"Dad ... I have to, uhm, ask you about something Ida and I' wondering about ... Actually, we made a bet, well, maybe not exactly a bet since neither of us opposed, but..."

"Yeah, yeah, come to the point, what are you wondering about?" Joakim innocently replied, unaware the ticking bomb.

"Well, what are you and Mom actually doing? Have you become swingers, or something like that?"

Joakim freezes to ice, staring blankly at Jens as his thoughts desperately whirls, searching for a believable lie.

Damn... what the hell am I supposed to say? There's no point in denying it, but how the hell did they figure it out? We've been as discreet and cautious as possible. Well... I guess I'll have to try to explain the situation so they don't think we're just fooling around with everyone. There's not much of choice, I cannot see any other way ...

Now it's Joakim's turn to clear his throat. In one gulp, he finishes the last drop of beer, and a trickle finds its way through the corner of his mouth and down onto his shirt. The little mishap lightens the mood, and both of them laugh heartily at Joakim's clumsiness. The laughter feels liberating, and Joakim gathers himself again in a desperate attempt to appear completely unaware.

"I hear what you're saying, but I don't understand why you're asking something like that?"

Jens does not look completely satisfied with the situation. "We're just a little curious. You've made quite a few new friends in a short time, and besides ... you're going to parties much more often than before."

"But does that necessarily mean we're swingers, for heaven's sake?"

"Of course not, but it is somewhat suspicious after all. Besides, you've never been secretive about enjoying sex."

"Hmm, this isn't easy ... but, well, you've actually hit the nail on the head. I understand that there's no point in coming up with some twisted explanation. We've been swingers for almost two years, but I'd like to explain how it is. No details, and I don't think you want to hear them either, but just so you don't think we're sleeping around with everyone."

"We didn't think so either."

"Even if you might not believe it, the social aspect is just as important as the sex itself. In fact, we've made some really good friends in that world. It's a bonus that we didn't really anticipate, it came as a pleasant surprise."

"Well, I've met some of your new friends, and I just have to say they seem nice and normal in every way."

"At least the people we have met are actually regular, sensible people. And I also want to make it clear that I didn't force your mother into this in any way. True, I came up with the idea and pushed a little at the beginning, but now we're both equally involved."

"Yeah, I believe we would have noticed if it has been the opposite. Mom seems maybe more pleased and happier than ever."

Joakim smiled. "Thats true, but it's not all about sex. Many times, we engage in ordinary activities like trips, concerts, and such. For example, the upcoming safari in Kenya, we're going together with Karola and Kalle. It was the same when we were skinning in Åre last winter. We said we were there alone, but we actually shared a cabin with Gisela and Olle. We had a great time, skiing all day, and maybe a thing or two happened in the evenings," Joakim stifled a laugh.

Jens looked surprised at his dad. "What's so funny about that?"

"I was just thinking about how we had planned to introduce Gisela and Olle to you. It's not fun to lie, but we were going to say they lived in the house next door and that Olle and I were out shovelling snow at the same time. We started talking, and then we skied together for the rest of the week. It's almost true and sounds believable, right? Anyway, we didn't have to go through that charade since you haven't met them yet," Joakim concludes with a sheepish expression.

Jens shakes his head and joins in Joakim's laughter. "So, you lie to your children..."

"Well, admittedly, we've been a bit careless with the truth, but would it have been better if we had just outright told you what we were up to?"

Jens ponders for a moment and then responds with a hesitant tone, "Hmm... hard to say, probably not."

"Well, it seems like you're handling it well, but how do you think Ida will take it? Your mother will be completely devastated. I'm not really sure what's best ... but I don't want you to mention anything to Ida before we've talked to her."

"Sure, I'll keep quiet until then, but I don't think Mom needs to worry so much. Ida and I have had a very rational discussion, and she hasn't been either sad or upset."

"I'm not so worried myself, but like I said, your mother has been terrified of this. Her biggest fear was probably that Ida would think she's a really bad mother."

"No, that's not the case, at least not from my side. You're still the same parents as before, neither better nor worse," Jens concludes in a tone that gives hope for a happy outcome.

Before they separate for the night, the conversation returns to more neutral topics. Despite the revelation, the evening was not so crazy. The disaster scenario that Joakim originally feared did not occur, and to his surprise he realizes that he feels relieved after the revelation, finally an end to lies and excuses. Susanne doesn't notice when Joakim crawls into bed next to her. He doesn't try to wake her up, knowing that she would probably stay awake the rest of the night if she knew their secret was no longer a secret

Even though the worst worries had subsided, his mind felt overwhelmed by thoughts of what they could have done differently. Nevertheless, he finally manages to fall asleep. However, he wakes up early. Susanne is still sleeping peacefully and unaware when he quietly gets up and starts preparing breakfast. He anxiously ponders how to deliver the unwelcome news as gently as possible. Hmm, I don't really feel fresh, was it too much beer or just not enough sleep? I definitely need a big cup of coffee, and Susanne probably needs the same, even if she doesn't know it yet ...

As soon as Susanne rubs the sleep out of her eyes, he hands over a ham sandwich and a mug of steaming hot coffee. She lights up and looks happy, unaware of what awaits her. As she slowly wakes up, Joakim begins to tell her, starting with how he and Jens had an interesting conversation after she and Jens' girlfriend had gone to bed.

"It's good that you can confide in each other. What were you talking about?" she asks.

"Yeah… it's absolutely amazing that we can have a confidential conversation, but I could do without this," he replies.

"What? Don't tell him he suspects something?!"

Joakim nods slowly. It is more than a suspicion, or as they say in legal cases, the prosecutor has a strong case.

We are reasonable suspects. Lately they've become more and more convinced that we're swingers."

Susanne stares blankly ahead for a few seconds before she gathers herself. "Okay, you say 'they'. Am I to interpret that as Jens and Ida discussing this?" She takes a long breath and continues. "No, this doesn't feel good, not at all."

"Yes, they have talked, several times", says Joakim. "I don't know who brought it up first, but it's less important."

"You right, but I'm sure it was Ida. Anyway, what did you tell Jens? I can imagine that he doesn't make a big deal out of it. I wouldn't be surprised if he's a little curious himself. But Ida, how will she react? I'm afraid she will get really upset when she realizes their guesses are correct. Will she accept me as a mother after this … or us as parents at all?"

I know you have been especially worried about how Ida would react if we were exposed. I asked what she said when they talked about it, how she reacted. According to Jens, she doesn't think it's anything to worry about. They've had these thoughts for a while, and Jens emphasized that she wasn't sad or upset."

Susanne looks somewhat calmer as she thoughtfully continues: "Well... we have to trust that, even if it feels fragile... God, it would be so nice if we could both accept that we are adults and do what we want. when it comes to our sex life."

"Without going into details, I tried to explain how it works when we meet our swinger friends. I emphasized that we don't always have sex when we meet. Sometimes it's just like when we hang out with our other friends...except we're a little more open in our conversation. Mostly I talked about the social aspect and all the wonderful cozy friends we've made."

It's good that you emphasized the social aspect. After all, it's not all about sex. But to say that we're a bit open when we meet our fuck-buddies is a significant understatement. We don't exactly have any restrictions when we discussing sex. It could just as well be stamps collectors discussing their great interest. Oh, I'm getting off topic. What else did you say?" Susanne asks curiously.

"Well, what else did I say? I guess I was pretty general in my explanations, but I pointed out that the swinger lifestyle has actually added more excitement to our lives. I mentioned that it has spiced up our sex life, even when we I'm alone. Mostly I talked about our wonderful friends and how much fun it is, even when we're not having sex."

Susanne interrupts him with a satisfied face. "Yes, it is true. It has truly enriched our lives in many ways."

Joakim nods thoughtfully and continues, "I also pointed out that people in the swinger world often complain less than people in general."

"That's also true, at least when it's comes to our friends. Of course there are exceptions, but we prefer to avoid such people. But what the hell are we going to do about Ida? You said we were going to talk to her?"

"Yes, I said so, but I wonder if it might be better to let Jens start and we'll talk to her later. What do you think about that?"

"Hmm, it won't be easy no matter how we do it. Ugh, I get a stomach-ache just thinking about it, but maybe you're right, that it's better that Jens start and we talk to her a bit later."

"Okay, Let's see what he thinks about it."

"We'll do that," Susanne replies with a strained smile.

By lunchtime, they talk to Jens, and he takes on the task of being the messenger without complaining. Susanne immediately looks relieved, maybe the confrontation can be postponed a few days. It would give her the opportunity to think through her defence speech more thoroughly, if such a thing were needed?

But not everything is bleak ... The invitation from Sandra and Johan for a spa evening disperses their thoughts, and suddenly Susanne sits there with a contented smile.

"Nice to see you smile again. What are you thinking about?"

"I was thinking about the meeting tomorrow. 'Christmas group' is an apt description, and I don't mean Christmas flowers in a pot ...", Susanne giggles.

"Haha, that's funny. 'Christmas group' is exactly what it's supposed to be. Especially when Sandra and Johan are there ... By the way, do you know how many we will be?"

"We'll be four couples. We haven't met the other two couples before, didn't recognize their nicknames. The spa closes at ten, but they have booked a smaller suite in a nearby hotel where we can continue afterward, if we feel like it."

"That sounds really nice, it's great to have something to look forward to despite not being as secretive as we thought," says Joakim, shaking his head with amusement.

"By the way, Sandra also mentioned that we could sleep over in the suite, if we want to."

Later in the day, Jens talks to his sister, and her first comment aligns well with Jens' gut feeling. - Good for them, I would have been more surprised if they came out as religious...

Susanne smiles happily as Jens tells her.

"Oh, that's great, no major harm done. We can bring it up when we meet her later this week. I would have preferred to continue without your and Ida's knowledge, but at the same time, it feels liberating not to have to lie."

"It's alright, Mom," Jens says with a smile. He's shaking his head and giving her a big hug.

Susanne continues cheerfully. "Just think about it, if we have friends visiting, we can simply say that special guests are coming, and you two will definitely stay away. Well, ... it feels really good now."

The next day, with relieved minds, they head towards Uppsala and the awaited spa meeting. The spa facility is not very large but more than sufficient for the planned activities. Susanne and Joakim haven't met the other two couples, but they are as they thought also easy-going and friendly. After a hesitant start with some wine and social chit-chat in the hot tub, they soon engage in sex play. However, the water has its limitations, and one by one, they move from the pool to sofas and tables. Before Joakim throws himself into the playful activities, he pauses for a few seconds, savouring the sight. With a smile, he acknowledges that Susanne's earlier reflection is indeed accurate – 'Christmas group' is really an apt description.

After a couple of intense hours at the spa facility, the girl at the reception discreetly knocks on the door - it's time to finish. Luckily, the hotel is not far away and Johan and Sandra have already checked in. Without any further interruption, they continue where they left off. But they are immediately faced with a problem – the room's single double bed cannot possibly accommodate eight people ... At first, they all try to squeeze into the bed, which turns out to be overly optimistic. But with a little ingenuity the problem is solved. The girls take a seat in the bed, and the boys along the sides. The idea works better than expected. At the same time as the guys fuck the girls, they create their own snake pit. The arrangement is particularly appreciated by the boys; fuck and eye candy at the same time.

n the end, after playing in the double bed, only Sandra, Johan, Joakim and Susanne are left. Even though they've used up most of their energy during the evening's activities, it's hard to convince their brains that their bodies have had enough. But after a half-hearted attempt at sex, they realize it's time to give up and get some rest.

The enjoyable Christmas day ends with the four of them huddled together in the double bed for a few hours of much-needed sleep. Breakfast the next morning, however, will be memorable in several ways, but that's a whole other story ...

The winter weeks pass surprisingly quickly and winter finally gives way to the approaching spring. The bare ground patches grow and become greener with each passing day. The feelings of spring awaken and everything feels lighter - a proper sex party seems fitting. Most of the meetings during the winter have been threesomes with an extra guy, unfortunately single girls are relatively few and harder to attract. But rescue is not far away - as on order, a party invitation arrives. Karin and Klas, whom they met at Helena and Svante's, are planning a spring party together with some friends.

Sussane reads the email to Jokim. "The party is planned for the weekend around Ascension Day. They have rented a training center outside Gothenburg and expect twenty to twenty-five couples plus a few single guys."

"Outside of Gothenburg ... did they mention where?"

"No, just that it is south of Gothenburg. It will be a three-day event with accommodation and food, all at cost price.

Joakim laughs with childish enthusiasm. "Party for three days ... like in the fairy tales. It sounds very interesting; we don't have anything planned that far ahead, do we?"

"I don't think so, I'll check the calendar," replies Susanne.

Norwegians and a demanding dominatrix

A couple of weeks later, Susanne is sitting at the computer and suddenly lights up, "Look, we have more info about the Ascension Day party. It's very detailed, do you want to hear?"

"Absolutely, what are they saying?"

"They start with a few lines about how nice it would be to meet again, the rest is general information, and some practical details.

WELCOME TO A SPECTACULAR SPRING PARTY
For a cost of seven hundred kroner per person, you get, in addition to pleasant company, accommodation for three nights including full board for two days.

- *Friday: Breakfast, Lunch, and Dinner.*
- *Saturday: Breakfast, Lunch, and Dinner.*
- *Sunday: Breakfast and refreshments.*

For simplicity's sake, the same price applies regardless of which day you arrive. In addition to drinks for breakfast, everyone brings their desired drinks for the other meals. We would like to know in advance who can help with any of the following:

Building playrooms, setting up/clearing tables, washing dishes, fetching firewood, etc.

Things to consider: Bring bed linens, towels, and drinks for meals. Also, don't forget your favourite toys. You can use the refrigerators in kitchen for your personally goodies, and special dietary food. Sauna and hot tub will be available at Friday and Saturday evening. We want everyone to dress up for dinner, anything goes! And last but not least, we will set up a large, well-equipped playroom with many exciting gadgets ...

THURSDAY: *You are welcome from lunchtime (noon at the earliest). No special activities are planned for Thursday evening. Those who have the energy and desire can of course play in the playroom. If you just want to take it easy take it easy and recharge before Friday, it's fine to relax by the fire in the family room.*

FRIDAY: *We prepare for the evening as we like. Take a walk in the beautiful surroundings or visit the nearby village for a beer with good friends. It is also perfectly okay to stay and relax in the nice weather we have ordered. Lunch is served between 12-1pm. The highlight of the day is, of course, the joint dinner; we expect to sit down around 19.00. Dress code. Latex and leather or other suitable clothing.*

SATURDAY: Same program as Friday and if possible, we turn up the party temperature even more.

SUNDAY: Cleaning of own sleeping space, kitchen and shared spaces as playroom etc. We finish with coffee and snacks before heading back to everyday life

"It sounds fantastic, we should definitely sign up. What do you think we should help with?" Joakim asks.

"Well, I can do some work in the kitchen, and you can help with the playroom. I think you'll be more useful there than in the kitchen," she adds with a meaningful smile.

"Yeah, the kitchen isn't my strong suit, so I'm happy to help set up the playroom. It's probably good if we can leave already on Thursday, right?" Said Joakim.

"Since it's quite a drive, it would be nice to have the journey behind us. In that case, we can sleep in properly on Friday."

"In that case, we can have a late morning on Friday."

"We may not know many people apart from Karin and Klas, but it's usually nice to meet new acquaintances. It's really nice that it's several days. Maybe we can go to Gothenburg, or to the coast on Friday or Saturday if the weather is okay."

"Sounds like a good idea," agrees Susanne and continues. "It would be really nice with some decent weather, but even if the sun doesn't show up, it could still be a good weekend. I'm really looking forward to this."

Rarely had Ascension Day felt so welcome as this spring. After five long hours in the car, they finally approach the farm.

"Joakim, are we really on the right track The road is getting narrower and narrower, soon we will have to share the road with a bunch of cows."

"It wouldn't surprise me, but I'm pretty sure we're on the right track. The farm should be secluded, according to the GPS it's only a couple of kilometres to go. It'll be really nice to sink into a sofa and relax with a glass of wine. I don't think we'll have much sex tonight, or what do you say, ma'am?"

"It's probably going to be quiet; we'd better go to bed early so we're fresh tomorrow. Did you see Karin emailed the attendee list, almost fifty people. Apparently, there were some Norwegian couples too, I'm sure it'll be an interesting weekend."

Most were already in place when they arrived; many hang out on the couches and enjoy the peace and warmth of the open fire. There is a little caressing here and there, but nothing more than that happens on the sofas in front of the fire. A few, however, are eager to investigate the playroom, but even their encouraging mating calls don't get the weary group on the couch going. After some wine and socializing, Susanne and Joakim retire to the small room they share with Kajsa and Henrik.

The next morning, they wake up early to the sunbeams that the thin linen curtains fail to keep out. It's clear that Joakim is awake; his morning erection immediately catches Susanne's eye. It doesn't take long before they're in the midst of a gentle morning fuck. The creaking bed soon wakes up their roommates, and after a while, they're also at it. Their joint efforts rub off; after a few more minutes, they can clearly hear that at least one of the Norwegian couples in the adjacent room has followed their example. When the bed squeaking eventually subsides, a couple of happy, lively faces look up and thank Susanne and Joakim for the pleasant wake-up call.

Yesterday's rain-heavy clouds have been replaced by blue skies and mild winds that give a taste of summer. Susanne and Joakim put on their running shoes and are pleased to see that their roommates have the same plans. Together, they go for a jog in the delicate May greenery. They jog at a leisurely pace along the narrow gravel road where the dew drops still glisten in the tufts of grass. The beautiful early summer morning and the looming party in the evening make their feet light. All everyday worries seem to be blown away; only the present moment exists. After a couple of kilometres, however, it doesn't feel as easy anymore, and all four turn back towards the farm.

After the morning chores are done, they go with Kajsa and Henrik to the nearby village. Restaurants and outdoor seating have opened their doors, probably just thanks to the excellent weather. The stores are selling off what was not sold last fall; the whole village seems to be waking up from its winter sleep. It doesn't take long until they find a happy group charging for the evening party at an outdoor terrace along the water. The outdoor bar group at the outdoor bar is enjoying the relatively warm spring sun. They sit down, order and join in the happy conversation, and as always ... a cold beer always tastes better in the company of good friends. After the beer, there will be more sightseeing and shopping, ending with an excellent seafood lunch before returning to the farm.

There they are met by a beautiful sight; the lawn between the houses is filled with sunbathing naturists, the yard has suddenly turned into a miniature Cap d'Agde. Most are just enjoying the sun and the heat, but some are already into the evening activities. Especially the Norwegians are in a good party mood; they fuck, toast and shout out their well-being, as if their national day never ended. Many Swedes are drawn into and share the Norwegian party atmosphere. The rest of the afternoon quickly disappears in a pleasant mixture of sex, laughter and happy antics.

However, it's still early in May; the shadows, which are growing longer, eventually cover most of the lawn between the houses. The dropping temperature, along with the setting sun, force even the most devoted party animals give up. It's now high time to prepare for dinner. With joint efforts, food is prepared while the great hall is set, and finally, everyone can settle down at the long tables. The atmosphere is at its best, it echoes with laughter and toasts to the party organizers. Most people have really taken to heart the advice to dress up to the teeth; black latex or leather creations in various forms are undoubtedly the most popular outfits.

However, a few women in red or blue corsets lighten up the otherwise somewhat dark choice of clothing. Many are BDSM-inspired; whips and handcuffs are worn by both women and men. Some of the women also wear collars that might be better suited for human's best friend. One of the couples takes it a step further; the man leads his partner to the table on a short leather leash. She obediently follows her master, but when it's time to sit down at the table, after all, she gets the responsibility of holding the leash.

Although there is no table placement, many couples voluntarily split up. The chatter quickly reaches a deafening level, interrupted only by drinking chants. Before the main course is even ready, most people have become very familiar with their table neighbours. At some of the tables, the acquaintance goes even further. Several couples finish the dinner with playful sex, plates and glasses have to give way and the rice table has to endure a rough treatment. However, the other dinner guests are not significantly disturbed by the eager couple and calmly finish with coffee and cake. After a while, most of them have disappeared to the playroom or just gone out and had a cigarette in the warm early summer evening. Susanne and Joakim reunite after dinner.

"Joakim, come on, I want to see what the Norwegians are up to. They've been doing this since this morning. What a pace, I don't understand how they can take it."

"I agree, it's time to get to know our Nordic neighbours a little better.

"It's a lot of attractive couples, and the lust is not lacking."

Susanne and Joakim are welcomed with open arms. With heart and soul, they join the Norwegian snake pit. Afterwards, they relax on the sofas in the great room, where it is still relatively quiet.

"God, they're wild." Joakim laughs and continues. "It was so damn nice to just let my hands roam around and be touched here and there."

"Yeah, I saw you liked it." Susanne suddenly falls silent and then continues in a completely different tone. "Did you have sex with the blonde girl without a condom?"

"Uhm…it just happened. I know it was stupid. She stopped me as I reached for the condom. I should have insisted, but…" Joakim shrugged. "Yup, I succumbed to temptation."

"It was actually stupid…really stupid! We have to be able to trust each other, it doesn't feel good when things like this happen."

"I understand, but after all, it wasn't the end of the world…"

Susanne stood up. "This made me lose my appetite for sex. I'll take a break, or go to bed. Then you can continue having sex without a condom."

"But for God's sake! Can't we talk about this? I promise to think twice from now on."
Susanne was quiet for a long time before she finally opened her mouth. "Okay, I'll stay for a while, but I don't think I want any more sex, with you or anyone else."

Susanne is angry, and Joakim feels guilty; the reconciliation attempt does not go well and the evening continues on a low mood. Not even a moment in the hot tub with a bunch of happy Gothenburg's can bring the party mood back. Finally, they both realize that there is only one sensible option left; they make their exit and go to bed with the hope that tomorrow will be better.

The next morning it's Susanne and Joakim's turn to wake up to the bed's creaking and lust-filled moans. Their roommates' loving sex act does not go unnoticed and after a while, Joakim creeps up on Susanne and they are soon in the middle of a passionate reconciliation act. Afterwards, when they catch their breath in each other's arms they see yesterday's events in a different light. Joakim assures Susanne that safe sex is the only way forward, and Susanne admits that she may have been overly harsh in her judgement.

Kajsa and Henrik's positive mood rubs off on them and yesterday's troubles soon disappear in the sun's gentle morning rays. It's still chilly outside, but the smell of damp grass confirms that summer is on its way. Outside, the silence is total except for some bird chirping; yesterday's hustle and bustle feel distant.

Neither the Norwegians nor anyone else has mustered the energy to get up on feet; it is a quiet and pleasant breakfast in the spring sun. Today jogging is put aside, instead they choose a slow walk along the narrow dirt road that winds past small farms and summer cottages, nestled in the fragile spring greenery.

When they come back, most people are already up, except for the Norwegian friends who are still recovering from yesterday's effort. A few sun-worshipping couples have already parked themselves on the lawn to get some colour on their winter-pale bodies. The sun's warming rays awaken the desire, it will be a light-hearted afternoon with happy pranks in the sign of eroticism. To everyone's delight, some energetic volunteers set up an impromptu shaving station in the sun. However, the idea is not to make the guys' chins smooth and fine; the target audience is undoubtedly those who have neglected shaving their nether regions.

After yesterday's fraternization, Saturday night's sex activity gets off to a flying start. As soon as dinner is over, most people move straight to the playroom; the foreplay is long over. Mattresses, sofas and swings are soon filled with horny women and men. There are constellations of all kinds, ranging from lone pairs to five, six pesos tightly intertwined. Blissful moans and orgasmic screams mix with laughter and happy conversations in a liberating mix. Joakim waits impatiently for Susanne in the playroom, but after a while he heads back to the dining room; maybe she is stuck in a protracted social discussion?

However, he does not get far; in the corridor he meets Susanne and her table neighbour from dinner. Hand in hand, the two women move determinedly towards the playroom. Joakim is about to ask what's going on, but his question remains a thought when he sees the strap-on dildo dangling from the woman's hand.

"Joakim, this is Camilla, she will ..."

Susanne is immediately interrupted. "Sorry Joakim, this is actually just for Susanne."

"Oh...", answers Joakim confused as the girls disappear into the playroom.

Camilla quickly slips into the dildo's leather harness, adjusts a few buckles and suddenly the temporary sex change is complete. In one fell swoop, Camilla changes;

suddenly she has turned into a strict and demanding dominatrix. She points at the mattress with a short whip. Susanne drops to her knees, stares in amazement at the thick dildo that sways provocatively in front of her eyes. Oh, what have I gotten myself into? I guess I missed this with the size, but…

"Hurry up, stop daydreaming and make sure your sweet pussy is ready for me," Camilla's commanding voice interrupts.

Susanne smiles at the game and sinks obediently down on the mattress. With poorly concealed eagerness, she follows Camilla's instructions. For a brief moment, she worries about losing control of the situation but soon realizes that she is looking forward to not being in charge. Eventually, Camilla's patience runs out; the non-existent foreplay is over before it started.

Susanne stares expectantly at Camilla as she slowly pushes the black, shiny object into her pubis. God, it feels like it's filling up my whole being, can I handle this?

Carefully but extremely purposefully, Camilla lets the dildo do its job until Susanne can no longer be passive. It's the signal Camilla has been waiting for; with a lustful smile she shifts into a higher gear. A veil of surprise quickly passes over Susanne's face before she once again loses herself in the pleasure that embraces her.

With her eyes fixed on Susanne, Camilla hisses. "You have to look me in the eyes, even when you come you have to look at me…" She raises her voice when there is no answer. "Susanne, can you hear me?"

"Uhm, it's not far away, Camilla, please..."

After another couple of painful minutes, or rather an eternity in Susanne's mind she finally gets to enjoy the sweetness of orgasm. Camilla slows down her powerful thrusts and turns to showering Susanne with caresses and kisses.

As soon as Susanne comes back from the land of ecstasy, she looks for Joakim's eyes, she takes gratefully accepts his help to sit up on the sofa. "Did you see what Camilla did to me?"

"Oh yeah, I saw, I couldn't for the life of me stop watching, but yeah...watching is a gross understatement; I probably stared like an idiot. You guys were absolutely insane, it was so damn wonderful watching your show, and it was clear that it wasn't just Camilla who was enjoying it."

Susanne smiled and shrugged. "It was an experience I absolutely wouldn't want to be without. At first, I didn't really believe that rubber dick; it was probably mostly my curiosity that was piqued, but then something happened..."

"I noticed," Joakim smiled.

Susanne turned to Camilla, "I was completely taken aback when you started. You knew how to turn me on; for a while it felt like I was going crazy."

"Yeah, I think I hit the right button, didn't I? It was really nice; I'd love to do it again sometime, and I don't think the audience would mind either," Camilla says with a wink at Joakim.

"Absolutely not, if you do it again, I'll definitely have to be there."

"I don't know where Micke, my sweet man, hangs out. I'll see if I can find him. Kisses to you both in the meantime," Camilla excuses herself and disappears towards the kitchen.

"Susanne, I got so damn horny I could hardly stand still. You say you're not interested in girls, but apparently you are, at least sometimes."

Well, I never think of girls that way, but I obviously don't have a hard time turning on, if it's the right girl. What happens, happens in the heat of the moment, so to speak. I don't want to sound innocent, but it was actually Camilla who took the initiative, but to be honest, maybe I wasn't too hard to persuade when she told me what she wanted to do." Says Susanne and shrugs her shoulders apologetically.

It was probably not the first time Camilla seduced an *innocent* girl.

"Absolutely, she definitely knew what buttons to push." Susanne smiled as she continued. "But I don't know if I'm so innocent..."

"No, it's been a long time since you crossed that line. I don't know if you noticed but Camilla enjoyed it at least as much as you did, she's probably more bi than you are, don't you think?"

"Maybe, but I don't really want to label myself as bisexual. I feel more like just sexual, and I mean sexual without any prefixes. I'm not really sure how to put it, but it feels like gender is less important What really matters is who you are as a person."

"I think I understand, it sounds reasonable," replies Joakim with a thoughtful tone.

"But what about you? How do you feel about men? Do you never turn a man on?"

"I don't see men that way, but I've definitely pushed the boundaries when it comes to gender identity. Although I've never been homophobic, I was very careful about what I touched when we first started in this world. Nowadays, I don't same respect for the male sex, if something happens in the heat of battle it's okay. It's actually pretty nice not to care who touches who, or what ..."

"Absolutely, to fully indulge in sex is wonderful. By the way, you said you were really horny, and you still are?"

Joakim looked questioningly at Susanne. "Sure, what goes on in your dirty mind?"

"It would be a shame if we missed Karin and Klas; they wrote that it would be nice to meet again, so maybe we could get intimate with them. But first I have to unwind, can't we just sit in front of the fire and cozy up a bit, just you and I?"

"Sounds like a good plan." Joakims agrees

"I'm just going to wash and put on my make-up; I'll probably need that after Camilla's treatment."

"Good idea, you look freshly fucked. There's not much lipstick left, and you have a very messy hairdo," confirms Joakim with a hearty laugh.

After they recover in front of the crackling fire, they go back to the playroom to find Karin and Klas. They hear Kla's voice from a group of horrified onlookers where a pair of legs stick up at head height. Legs in the air is not uncommon in these situations, but... in this case, the woman has traded her porn boots for a pair of normal slalom boots. The boots are securely anchored to a wooden beam at approximately half a meter interval. The strong beam is attached to a steel cable that disappears into an electric winch in the ceiling.

"Ahh, now I get it," says Joakim. I saw the ski boots earlier, but I didn't understand what they were doing here.
Susanne nods, "I saw them too, but I didn't understand either, it's not exactly obvious ..."

With a push of a button from Klas, the winch whizzes and the woman in boots stops at shoulder height. After he ensures safety and that the "victim" is on the notes, he tackles the task enthusiastically. He lets the plugged-in, oversized massage wand gently slide back and forth in the slit that sways provocatively right in front of his eyes. Like an attentive conductor, he lets the woman's contented moans dictate the intensity of the vibrations until she struggles to stay still. She writhes and thrashes her arms until she finally gives up with a drawn-out moan to the wand's relentless vibrations. Klas recklessly continues the treatment but suddenly stops, glances at his wristwatch and suddenly stops the treatment.

"Sorry baby, now I have to let you come down. More than four minutes with your head down is not recommended."

Disappointed sighs mix with spontaneous applause as the woman is slowly lowered to the floor. Klas helps her off with the ski boots and makes an attempt to leave the playroom, but before he disappears into the crowd, he is stopped by Joakim.

"Do you know where Karin is? Susanne and I thought it would be nice if we could have a repeat of the cozy time we had at Helena and Svante's?"

"Sure thing," Klas responds, beaming. "I'm sure Karin would appreciate it; you guys took such good care of her in Stockholm. But I'm not sure where she's gone; maybe she's out having a smoke."

Sure enough, Karin had joined the others in dire need of *fresh air*." However, she immediately stubs out her cigarette when she hears the plan. They find a secluded corner where they together make an effort to reach the heights of their first meeting in Stockholm. Afterwards, a rosy-cheeked Karin hugs them both and announces with bubbly enthusiasm.

"Now I'm definitely excited to organize another party!" She falls silent for a second and then adds cheerfully, "maybe already in the fall, right Klas?"

"Well, maybe, if we can get enough people together..."

"Count us in," Susanne responds just as enthusiastically, and Joakim nods with a satisfied smile.

However, the evening is coming to an end; even though it's not midnight yet, the party is winding down. Suddenly both the sofas in front of the fire and the kitchen have become more popular than the playroom; most people apparently burned out their energy yesterday. Even the Norwegians are not very active, and the previously massive soundscape of lustful moans and laughter has softened considerably. Even Susanne and Joakim have lost their momentum and end the evening in the hot tub together with other tired and seemingly satisfied party animals. The summer heat hasn't quite arrived yet, but the warm water keeps the increasingly chilly early summer night at bay. There is a relaxed and contented atmosphere in the overcrowded hot tub, happy faces and happy laughter are washed down with the last sips of beer and wine. Everyone in the hot tub agrees that more parties like this are needed. Words of appreciation and toasts are once again raised to the party organizers and their excellent initiative.

Although the late alcohol consumption is noticeable, they are satisfied with yesterday's efforts. But this morning no one insists on neither jogging nor walking; not even a quick fuck is on the agenda. As soon as breakfast is over, they clean the bedroom and start packing, but where are all their things? As usual, clothes and toys are scattered here and there, but after a tour of the play-rooms, they can finally close their suitcases. Then they start cleaning the common areas, this also feels like a pleasant task thanks to all the wonderful people.

Trouble at the Club

Spring goes by fast and the summer holidays are approaching. Susanne smiles happily as she gets behind the wheel of the packed car. "I love being at home, but it's wonderful to go on vacation but there will be many miles on the roads ..."

Well, around five hundred kilometres round trip because we take the detour across Holland; but at least we save a few miles thanks to the ferry," replies Joakim with a satisfied smile.

"We should be at the hotel pretty early. It would be nice if we could take it easy before we go to the club."

"That would be nice, as long as there isn't too much road work on the highway we'll be there in the early afternoon."

Although the cabin, which was spartanly furnished, was on the lower deck, it still felt like a touch of luxury, a luxury that would provide a few hours of much-needed sleep. It was a quiet evening, just dinner and a glass of wine and then quickly to bed. After an early breakfast, they are ready to face the hectic pace of the German autobahns, as usual the cruise control was of little help. The frequent road works caused the speed to oscillate between extremes. Despite this speed rollercoaster, the six hundred kilometres journey from the port of Travemünde to the small Dutch town of Moordrecht went without any major problems. After check in they even managed a short walk in the small community before preparations for the club visit began. Eager and curious, they look forward to the evening. Fun4Two has a solid reputation as Europe's best swingers club, and soon they will find out if it lives up to its reputation.

"Joakim, did you notice his smile when we checked in? He probably had no doubt why we came here. Can there be so many other reasons to stop in Moordrecht, besides visiting the club?"

"Probably not, but the Dutch are known for being open-minded. He probably has no problem with their guests visiting the club. Maybe we'll even see him there? Must be damn nice to have a club like 'Fun' within easy reach." "

"In any case, it will be interesting to see if it is as good as everyone claims. This feels like one of the most important items on our bucket list."
Joakim looks up in surprise. "Bucket list, do we have such a list?"

"At least I have one in my head, but maybe we should put it down on paper?"

"Okay, what do you have on your list, or do you possibly have two lists, an official one and one for sex-related activities?"

"Hmm, good question …" Susanne replies thoughtfully and continues. "We have plenty of time, so maybe we should write down some items on the 'sex list'. It doesn't necessarily have to be thought out, just a little brainstorming to start with, then we can get more serious in the next step."

You know that men think with their dick, so brainstorming is perfect in this context, laughs Joakim."

"Well, let's have a glass of wine and write down some suggestions separately. If I know both of us well, we'll probably come up with similar ideas, don't you think?"

"Sure, but maybe we should only bring fantasies and desires that are reasonably realistic, right?"

"Absolutely, there will probably still be a lot of crazy ideas ..."

After a glass of wine, they each have their list of imaginative suggestions. Susanne smiles when she compares her own list with Joakim's. "Hmm, fewer than I thought, does that mean we've already fulfilled most of our fantasies?"

"It seems so, but we probably have more things to check off than these. Some proposals may be more difficult to implement than others," Joakim points out. "For example, a threesome with a shemale. That would be nice but maybe not so easy to fulfill?"

"Probably not. I'm not sure how we're going to find a suitable candidate, maybe in Cap? The big problem is finding someone we feel comfortable with, and who's actually feminine and attractive. We'll probably get back to that point ... " She pauses for a second before continuing. "Or maybe some things should remain fantasies."

Joakim nods, "you might be right. "

Susanne breaks into a big smile as she reads the next paragraph on Joakims list. "This one is a highlight; oil party sounds both realistic and wonderful."

Joakim confirms Susanne's words with a satisfied grin. "Good suggestion, I guess you agree? I also like the next point. Swingers cruise certainly has a place on the list, but it will probably be an expensive trip."

"Sure, but let's prioritize what feels important but we won't have time for this right now. At least, I have to start getting ready. It's almost eight o'clock."

They freshen up and try on different outfits. Do these shoes fit well? Red or black? Are thigh high boots better? The end result for Susanne is an elegant leather dress with matching shoes. Joakim is, like most guys in these contexts, often more well-dressed than sexy.

They are waiting for the taxi in the hotel lobby. Once in the car, the driver asks for the address. Joakim's answer becomes a counter question. "Do we really need to give you an address?"

The driver just smiles and replies, "I'm pretty sure where you want to go ..."

No more is said about the destination and after a few minutes they drive through Fun4Two's large iron gates, usually closed to prevent curious and unannounced guests. They check in and after a short visit to the changing room find themselves in the bar. One of the club's successful elements is the all-inclusive concept. All food and drinks are included in the entry fee, so there's no need to keep track of money or drink tickets. They can simply start with an aperitif of their choice and then move on to the tasty buffet.

Although drinks, including alcoholic ones, were included in the entrance fee, it does not seem to cause any major problems. Most people are obviously aware that sex and excessive alcohol consumption are not a good combo. Early in the evening, the club is not that different from a regular restaurant, except for the more daring dress of the ladies. But at around 22:00 the picture changes. From then only sexy outfits are allowed. The amount of exposed skin increases significantly, and those who have not fully grasped the meaning of this soon realize that they are not in an ordinary dance hall. Most women manage to meet the club's demands for an erotic dress code with an emphasis on style. The men's, however, have a harder time living up to the requirement, but most men still dress tastefully.

After the delicious buffet Joakim stands in line at the bar. Despite the staff's efforts to take care of all orders, things are slow. He passes the time by discreetly spying on the women around him, but his discretion is not very successful. The woman next to him soon notices his gaze and returns his interest with a smile filled with sensuality. A lively conversation quickly ensues and Joakim momentarily forgets his original purpose. A continuation with the woman in the playrooms feels both enticing and realistic.

Susanne, who has been waiting at the table, eventually becomes curious as to why the promised drink never arrives and makes her way to the bar. "Joakim, what's going on with our drinks?"

No answer, no reaction ... Joakim is well on his way to drowning in the Dutch woman's sensual gaze and has temporarily shut out the outside world. Susanne tries again, but without noticeable results. It is only when she taps Joakim on the back that he becomes aware of her existence.

He mumbles a "coming soon" but immediately goes back to conversing with the woman at his side. That is the breaking point. Susanne hisses angrily: "I don't give a damn about you" and turns on her heel.

Only then does the bubble burst, Joakim apologizes to the Dutchman and rushes after Susanne.

"Well, now I'm worth talking to," says Susanne with a sour expression. "I will not tolerate being ignored as if I were invisible."

"Sorry, that's not what I meant. I was just so fascinated by that woman."

"Oh thanks, I noticed that!"

"I didn't actually approach her. I was just flattered that a slightly younger, attractive woman showed interest in me."

"I understand, but it wasn't just that you weren't paying attention to me. You didn't even notice I was talking to you

as it just because I didn't listen to you, or were you a little jealous too?"

"No, I don't think so. I was just so damn disappointed when you completely ignored me. I was like air, but… hmm, maybe a little jealous too." Suddenly she lights up with a fleeting smile. "After all, I have to agree with you on one thing: she looked damn good."

"Anyway, that was clumsy and insensitive. I'm really sorry. This didn't start well, let's try to get back in the mood. Let's get that drink that should have been here already, and then we'll go up upstairs checking out the playrooms, what do you think my dear?"

"Oh, so I'm your sweetheart again… But you're right, let's forget about this. I'll skip the drink, get me a glass of white wine instead." She pauses for a few seconds and adds in a sarcastic tone, "It might go faster than the drink that spilled …or wherever it went."

A little wine and small talk lighten the mood and after a while Susanne suggests that they take a look in the playrooms. They go upstairs via the spiral staircase from the dance floor and suddenly find themselves in the middle of moaning and gasping men and women. The saying; From the ashes to the fire, has rarely been more appropriate, the event in the bar is soon forgotten in the erotic atmosphere. Susanne takes a seat on a massage table and within just a couple of minutes several couples gather around them like flies to a sugar cube.

Somewhat worried, she makes eye contact with Joakim, who reassures her with a confirming nod – I'm here, just lay back and enjoy. Five or six people caress her while she takes care of the low-hanging fruit just an arm's length away. Joakim also participates in the orgy, but his gaze remains firmly fixed on Susanne's sensual face, which glows with desire, but that is only the beginning. Soon Susanne's whole body radiates with ecstasy and desire and gives in to the sex rush that is well on its way to completely taking over her senses. With one hand on Susanne and the other in the panties of the German woman at the side, Joakim is inclined to join in paying tribute to the club. The woman who slowly jerks him also lets Susanne share in her caressing touch.

But all is not as it seems ... Soon he discovers that the woman actually has both hands at Susanne's body. Surprised, he realizes that it is actually the German woman's partner who is doing her best to satisfy him. With an open mind he tries to embrace the pleasure but fails. He apologizes and moves to the other side of the bench.

However, Susanne does not know about Joakim's dilemma. She is in her own bubble and is approaching climax at rocket speed. With wide, unfocused eyes, she stares at the ceiling as ecstasy washes over her. Afterwards, she calmly remains on the bench, with no plans to leave the wonderful place. With a shameless smile, she closes her eyes and eagerly awaits what comes next.

A middle-aged French man takes over, clearly versed in how best to please a woman with the help of his fingers. In less than thirty seconds he sends Susanne back to the realm of ultimate pleasure. She shakes uncontrollably, but Joakim holds her tight until the orgasm subsides. Dazed, she gets up from the bench, thanks the dexterous man with a hug, and then sinks into Joakim's waiting arms.

"My God, that guy really knew how to use his fingers. You just have to learn. Come on, let's go somewhere where we can be undisturbed. I can try to explain how he did it."

"I saw that it worked. It didn't take you more than a few seconds to climax. I'm all ears. How on earth did he do it?"

Susanne explains, Joakim listens and tries. After a few failed attempts, it suddenly works ...

Afterwards, Joakim gives a satisfied smile "Great, that's exactly what he did. I think a lot of women would like that, try it if we find a nice couple."

The club is crowded and the evening still has more adventures to offer. The French/English couple on the adjacent bed wastes no time in reciprocating Susanne's invitation and soon a change of partners takes place. Joakim tests his newfound skills and the woman confirms with a satisfied "Oh honey, I must say you have clever fingers..." Afterwards, with newfound confidence, they move on to the next room where two Dutch couples are fully engaged in playful sex. Susanne and Joakim are welcomed with open arms and the Dutch couples willingly show off their best assets, or rather their best body parts. Despite the less successful start, they feel more than satisfied with the evening. The club is highly praised and a return visit is a definite item on their bucket list.

The next day, their journey continues on worn highways through the Netherlands and Belgium. However, road conditions improve considerably when they eventually reach the expensive but pleasant toll roads of France. After another overnight stop along the way, they find themselves once again in the "Big Apple" of sin. What surprises await them this time? Could it possibly surpass their previous visit to paradise?

Back to Cap

Once again Cap d'Agde opens its doors. After the usual arrival process, they hang up their travel clothes in the wardrobe and enjoy the sweetness of naturism. The first two days they relax on the swinger beach without any major exaggerations. On the third day, the calm is interrupted when they are joined by a lively gang from southern Sweden and a couple from Stockholm. The beach literature that has been started can stay in the bag for the time being; all attempts at reading are made impossible by the happy and horny group. There is playful sex here and there, while the discussions alternate between serious and less serious topics. The atmosphere is top notch and baguettes and snacks are washed down with sparkling wine and beer from the coolers. Susanne and Joakim quickly become part of the community and when they leave the beach for the day, both get the feeling of being part of an odd but nice extended family.

The next day Joakim wakes up with a breakfast tray on the bedside table and a congratulatory greeting. He has the gift Susanne smuggled from home and adds with a knowing smile, "This may not be very exciting, but you may have other wishes for your birthday."

Joakim immediately lights up. "You know what I wish for, don't you?"

"I think I do ..." Susanne replies with a matching smile.

Around lunchtime, the whole group gathers again on the crowded swinger beach. Susanne enjoys being with her female friends; the girls have really found each other. Just like yesterday, the dialogue is characterized by intimate conversations and happy laughter. After a while, Susanne stands up and passes the cool champagne around.

"Let's toast and congratulate Joakim, it's his birthday today!"

All the Swedes stands up, toasts, cheers and starts singing Happy Birthday to you ... Several of the couples around raise their glasses and happily join in the congratulations in different languages. Joakim smiles contentedly at Susanne's initiative.

Unusual but nice to celebrate naked, surrounded by lots of other naked people These are the days that enrich life.

The celebration eventually subsides, Joakim thanks for the attention and he returns to a lying position under the parasol. That's when it happens, on a discreet order from Susanne, four women throw themselves at the unsuspecting Joakim. Susanne catches a glimpse of Joakim's equally surprised and happy smile before he more or less disappears under the pile of naked women. A pair of soft lips closed around his cock, which rose gratefully. A condom is rolled on, and before he knows it, the dick is in familiar surroundings. He can't tell which of the women is riding him, but at the moment it feels less important. His attention is directed instead to the woman straddling his chest. The seductive scent of her well-groomed sex right in front of his eyes effectively shuts out all irrelevant thoughts. As he buries his face in the glory before him, he feels the change. A new rider takes over and continues the ride at the same intense pace as her predecessor.

For the unusualness he thanks the condom, without this otherwise boring but necessary item the fun would have ended far too quickly. For a few too short minutes, the participants take turns pleasing Joakim, who gratefully accepts the attention. He fights valiantly to stay in the wet dream that has suddenly and joyfully turned into reality. But happiness is fleeting, and even faster than it came, the condom is torn off and replaced by a pair of lips working frantically. Although Joakim does what he can, the treatment soon demands its reward.

Susanne does not participate in the courtship herself; she has instead taken on the task of keeping an eye out for the beach police. But say the happiness that lasts ... these true words also applied to the courtship of the ladies. It's all over in less than ten minutes.

A blushing and panting Joakim shuffles up to a half-sitting position and shouts: "Great thanks to all the wonderful ladies, and especially you Susanne. It feels like I've woken up from a dream, a really wet one. But without doubt, the best present ever. You really knew what I wanted," he laughs happily and embraces Susanne in a hearty hug.

"It wasn't that hard to figure out. I think a lot of guys would have enjoyed such a courtship," adds Susanne with a mischievous smile. "And probably many girls too ..."

Joakim soon recovers but cannot stop reflecting on what happened. He asks Susanne to fill in any details he may have missed. "It was crazy fun, were there many curious people?"

"Sure, it caused quite a stir, both couples and single guys watching. I heard a lot of appreciative comments. I myself kept an eye on the surroundings; we didn't want any police here. But we were lucky they weren't. here to-day."

Joakim shakes his head. "Those who saw me must have wondered why I got such treatment. I don't look like a good-looking actor, and no one can accuse me of being a bodybuilder. They must have thought that either I was blessed with a big dick or that I have a fat wallet." He sighs, "it's not even lunch, how the hell is this birthday going to end?"

"Well, this is going to be hard to top, but we'll see to-night. I think everyone's going out to eat and Karin man-aged to book a table at pizzeria Flora. Afterwards it's go-ing to be a club, or we'll continue at someone's apart-ment, hopefully someone with more space than we have.

You might expect more attention from the girls, but maybe that's ok?

"Absolutely," replies Joakim with a satisfied smile.

A simple but pleasant dinner at pizzeria Flora is followed by a visit to one of the free clubs. That is, free for couples, while single guys have to pay a hefty initiation fee, which with any luck can result in a lay. If a couple does not want any help from the single guys, a simple "no, thank you" is enough. But if the lady in question wants to be extra pampered by one or more guys, there are good opportunities for that. In that case, it's only her desires or, possibly, the intimate parts of the body that set the limits ...

To Joakim's delight, the evening continues at the club in the same spirit as on the beach. Susanne is also satisfied as she no longer has to watch out for the police and can accompany the rest of the congratulators who take care of Joakim.

The next day there is a late awakening, only around lunchtime they head to the swinger beach. For them, it will be a significantly calmer day compared to yesterday, now it's sun and swimming that dominate the activities. The only disturbances are some stubborn vendors and the beach bums handing out flyers to the clubs. Suddenly, Susanne has a flyer in her hand.

"Joakim, look at this. Glamor has foam parties. Doesn't that sound interesting?"

"Really, today?"

"Yup, and every other day of the week between 2 and 7 p.m. Outside in the courtyard. Forty euros per couple, shouldn't we try and see how it is? It's nearly twelve-thirty, so it might be a good time to go there right after lunch It shouldn't be a problem to bring this crazy bunch along, right?"

"I can't imagine it would be," Joakim responds, handing the flyer to Klas.

The assumption turns out to be correct. finally, they become five couples who feels for playing in the foam. Just before 2 p.m., they join the line of expectant people outside Glamour. After only a few minutes in the winding line, a suggestive scent creeps up on them, a concoction of sunscreen, perfume and sweat. The distinct smell amplifies the already annoying itch in their groin, impatiently they waiting for the gates to Glamour's dazzling white walls to open. After another ten long minutes in the blazing sun, they finally reach the entrance. But before they are allowed in, they have to attend to practical formalities. In addition to the entrance fee, most of their earthly belongings must be left in the cloakroom. Only the necessities of life are allowed into the scammer's paradise, in this case: money, condoms and cigarettes ...

Inside the premises, they quickly realize that the wait was worth it. The dance floor is full with naked, foam-covered bodies moving to the music while caressing their partner or any of the couples around them. At first glance, it seems that everyone is caressing and touching each other. The area inside the walls is spacious, with not only the dance floor and giant hot tub, but also a dozen PVC-covered beds. Most of these beds are placed in refreshing shade where one can rest or engage in other activities freely. Many clearly seek these little oases to satisfy the desires that body contact on the dance floor creates. Orgies are already underway in several places, laughter and moans of pleasure mix with the insistent, techno-influenced music. Susanne gets caught up in the light-hearted atmosphere and her thoughts drift away to ancient orgies.

God, the wild parties of the Romans couldn't have been so different if we ignored the slaves. Well, actually, there's probably not that much of a difference here either. Most of them are probably slaves to their own lust and who isn't ... but shit, everyone looks ridiculously happy, what kind of place is this?

With childlike enthusiasm they plunge into the foam, almost immediately engulfed like everyone else in a rush of ecstasy that cannot be attributed solely to the sparkling wine. The soft, caressing foam produces a strange mixture of erotic excitement and unadulterated joy. They give and take, neither they nor anyone else mind a playful caress on the bottom or other body parts. The laughter of about two hundred blessed women and men is priceless; even children's sparkling eyes on Christmas morning pale in comparison.

After a while the foam subsides, immediately replenished by the foam cannons on the roof. For a few minutes, large clouds of foam float down and quickly cover everything and everyone on the dance floor. The poor souls trapped under the foam cough and splutter for a while but soon return to the play. With fresh foam at shoulder height, the wild party continues with undiminished strength. Susanne and Joakim continue to bounce around to the intense techno beat but eventually take a break.

They catch their breath with a glass of rosé on the angry red PVC couch next to the dance floor. Suddenly, Susanne grabs a black, well-built man who is dancing past, but the effect is not quite what she expected. The man staggers and sits down on the couch, but only for a fraction of a second. The slippery PVC plastic causes him to continue down to the floor and disappear into the foam like a slippery bar of soap. Surprised, Susanne stares at her missing find, but soon lets out a sigh of relief when a lathered, laughing figure crawls back to the couch a few seconds later. She stammers an apology and gets a hug and a cheery response in French before the man returns to his partner on the dance floor.

There is a lot going on in the foam and a hot topic of conversation is the slim Spanish girl who rushes around like a whirlwind. One moment she crawls between people's legs and tastes what she finds. In the next second she's gone, on the way to a new low hanging fruit. But it's not just the Spanish girl who takes the initiative - both Susanne and Joakim slide around lazily in the foam. It's a great feeling to fill your hands with foam and then lather up a tantalizing bust, or a lovely tanned butt under the influence of the general euphoria on the dance floor.

Eventually they leave the foam and to their delight, Pontus and Maggan have managed to claim one of the large double beds in the shade. They settle down on the mattress and playful sex ensues. After a while, a woman with broken English asks if she can borrow a corner of the bed to rest. Joakim nods approvingly and Pontus waves invitingly, but the woman can only reply: "Sorry, too tired".

The tired woman sits down at the head of the bed and the game continues. After a few more minutes, Maggan notices a woman curiously watching their activities with a happy expression. Maggan catches her eye and gives the woman a warm smile. That becomes the starting signal, and the stranger immediately gets up and approaches them. With a distinct French accent, she asks somewhat shyly, "Is it okay to join?"

All four of them light up and nod happily. The newcomer immediately becomes the center of attention and is treated royally, or rather, queen-like. The tired Frenchwoman at the head of the bed observes with interest what is happening with the newcomer. After a while, desire triumphs over fatigue, and she also joins the play.

When everyone eventually collapses, sweaty but happy, the woman who initially joined them thanks them in broken English. "This was extraordinary." Then she breaks into a big smile and points at the other French woman. "We are sisters ..."

The four Swedes look a little puzzled at first, but soon join the sisters' happy giggles before the French women wave and disappear towards the bar, laughing.

A couple of days later, they are invited to Karin and Klas' home together with the other Swedes and a Spanish couple, Maria and José. Both seem nice and are also social and speak good English. After a light dinner, they immediately start with dessert, which in this case has little to do with food. Joakim and Klas take on Maria and José, while Susanne piques José's interest. At first, it's okay, but the charming Spaniard has a quirk - his biggest passion seems to be licking the ears of his sex partners

He constantly lets the tip of his tongue explore Susanne's ears. She shivers, unable to think of anything else and soon she begs him to stop, but his ear fetish is too strong, soon he is back, into Susanne's seemingly irresistible ears. That's the breaking point, she excuses herself to go to the toilet and slips out of the passionate Spaniard's arms. She finds Joakim, who is currently doing his best to please Maria. Unlike her husband, the Spanish woman clearly shows that she prefers a proper fuck instead of having her ears cleaned. Despite Joakim's commitment to the Spanish woman, he cannot avoid hearing Susanne's outrage. He apologizes and follows her out into the hallway.

"I understand. Maria is really charming, I'd love to stay but if you want to get out of here, of course I'll come with you. You probably had liked Maria better ..."

Together they walk the short distance to their apartment, sit on the balcony with a glass of wine and decide to continue at a club. Around midnight there is a knock on the door and Karin and Klas are also keen on a club visit, even though they continued to play with the Spaniards. Choosing a club is easy – Glamor is just five minutes from the Heliopolis complex, where both couples have their apartments. After a glass of wine on the balcony, all that remains is to freshen up the make-up and choose the right outfit. In a sudden whim, both women have minimized their outfits to just a corset and thigh-high boots. Klas and Joakim look puzzled at the women. "Are you really going to go like that?" Joakim asks with raised eyebrows.

"Are we overdressed or what do you mean?" replies Karin and stifles a bubbling laugh.
"Well, I'm not quite sure what I meant. But that's perfectly fine, of course; we're in the capital of sin, after all. I don't think anyone would have much of an objection to you forgetting your panties."

"On the contrary, you will get lots of compliments on your good taste in clothes," adds Klas.

He was righter than he realized - the women were showered with compliments and invitations from both men and women. Even Glamour's doormen, who aren't usually chatty, drop a few appreciative comments. The club offers the usual mix of people of all kinds and categories. Some are very attractive, while others are definitely not ones you would want to get intimate with. Together with Karin and Klas, they navigate through Glamour's endless corridors, in search of attractive couples, and they have good luck. On two occasions they catch attractive fish in their nets. But both times it's the French couple who don't feel like opening their mouths and revealing their broken English. On the other hand, without any hint of shame, they are happy to show what they like when it comes to sex. Looking forward to closing time and significantly richer in experiences of erotica à la française, they stagger home, tired but satisfied with the night's catch.

But as always ... even though two weeks feels like an eternity upon arrival, the days disappear at a rapid pace. The question is whether it would be successful to have another week with a daily rhythm that shifts more and more with each passing day. On their last evening, they decide to start at Pizzeria Flora. After a not too long wait, Madame herself waves and points to a couple of available seats while shouting an order at a waiter. The table neighbours one gets is, as usual, a lottery, but this evening they have hit the jackpot. The English couple is friendly, talkative, and about the same age as themselves. Although the woman dominates most of the conversation, it doesn't matter, both feel genuinely pleasant and easy-going. And as usual; Flora's busy staff serves a piping hot pizza that lives up to its appetizing smell once again. Susanne and Joakim happily conclude that it seems to be a successful end to their vacation.

The English couple also seems to enjoy the company, and Wanda suggests continuing the evening with a drink in their camper. The silent Brian, who apparently shares the same opinion, smiles and nods in agreement. The campground, which is within walking distance of the restaurant, is well-guarded, and diligent guards stop anyone who lacks the plastic bracelet that serves as proof of belonging there. With hesitant steps, they approach the entrance, but luck is on their side as the guard is fully occupied checking a packed car and its passengers.

Outside Wanda and Brian's camper, the conversation continues in a relaxed atmosphere with drinks and snacks. The topics shift between sex and everyday life in Sweden versus England, but increasingly gravitate towards the former subject. The erotic atmosphere thickens, and after a while, Wanda suggests they go inside not to disturb the neighbours. In the same moment the door closes, their few garments come off. Wanda and Joakim take the bed, followed shortly by Susanne and Brian. The bed creaks and protests under the weight of four people, but no one seems to take the warning signs seriously. Suddenly, it happens, something cracks, and the head end of the bed collapses with a loud crash into the camper's storage space. What started so promisingly comes to an abrupt end.

Fortunately, no one gets hurt, but all sexual activity stops the moment the bed collapses. All four of them are hit by a hysterical fit of laughter that quickly and effectively kills the sexual mood. Further sex activities have to be postponed of practical reasons as the bed is currently unusable. They briefly consider moving to Susanne and Joakim's apartment, but with laughter still bubbling in their throats, a restart feels distant. A glass of wine feels more relevant at the moment than continued sexual endeavours. Wanda and Susanne stay outside the camper while Brian and Joakim investigate what happened to the bed. Luckily, it turns out that only one attachment came loose, clearly not meant to bear the weight of four adults during physical activity ...

With hopes of meeting their English friends again next year, they pack the car and leave Cap for this time. Joakim's courtship on the beach and Glamour's childishly fun foam parties have elevated the entire stay a notch. The countless hours in the car that await them feel bearable thanks to all the wonderful memories. However, it's not just memories that make them smile, they also look forward to meeting their new friends back home. The small world they initially glimpsed into is no longer that small. The horizon has widened considerably since their first stumbling steps into the swinger world.

Back in Sweden, the carefree summer days are coming to an end, autumn arrives with structure and routine. Friends have returned from vacations and country houses, everyone seems eager for parties, and several pleasant suggestions land in the mailbox. What stands out a little extra is undoubtedly the 17th-century masquerade planned for the autumn. The invitation boasting a grand castle-like building ignites the imagination. Even seven or eight couples of their closest friends are excited about the idea, so there are good chances for a successful event.

But... where do you find period-appropriate clothes without having to spend a small fortune? The rescue, as so many times before, is the blessed internet. After some clicking and jumping between different online stores, the problem with costumes and accessories is finally solved. Susanne will wear a minimal dress with a touch of the 18th century, along with a matching Marie Antoinette-style wig. Joakim settles for tight pants, a long velvet jacket, and a frilled shirt topped with a powdered wig in traditional style. With the practical details sorted out, all that's left is to count the days and look forward to the up-coming party.

Masquerade with an unusual pre-party

They stop in the courtyard in front of the old stone house, surprised and disappointed to find that the reality in no way matches the description they received in the invitation. Once upon a time, the building was probably the pride of the area, but that time is long gone. Yet... despite the obvious neglect, the old worn facade still exudes an untamed, timeless charm.

In the kitchen, the party organizers were already busy with preparations for tonight's dinner. There was no time for a long chat; they only got given a key and a short information about where to stay. On their way out, they peer curiously into the ballroom, not surprised to see that it too has fallen to decay. Even though time has taken its toll on both the facade and the interior, they can't help but smile, the house was definitely made for a decadent party. Back out in the sun, they find their accommodation, a smaller villa of a much younger vintage. They will spend the next two nights together with four other couples, the extended family from the happy days in Cap d'Agde reunited.

It is a joyous reunion, but there was no time for either social or sexual activities They quickly throw in their luggage and head off to tonight's dinner. Luckily, they don't have to spend time changing into silk and velvet this evening.

The social interaction they missed upon arrival becomes more intense during dinner. Everyone has something to share, from everyday family events to sexual encounters, all discussed with enthusiasm and curiosity.

Despite the nice dinner, it won't be a late night. When the food and drink were consumed, they went back to the house. Those who were hoping for sex were disappointed, it was just time for some small talk and a glass of wine before bed. The yawns were contagious and soon everyone in the house had retreated. After a short while only muffled snoring can be heard through the thin walls.

Susan and Joakim wake up to a low-key conversation in the kitchen, some were obviously earlier than themselves. The breakfast became long and pleasant, one that they rarely have time for at home. After a second round of coffee, the whole group takes a walk in the pleasant late summer weather. The country road, still dusty from summer in the autumn sun, soon leads them away from the farmhouses and barns. They enjoy the picturesque countryside at its best, with fields and meadows interspersed with small woodlands in a pleasant mix. The only thing that could possibly enhance the idyllic scene are the haystacks from bygone times. The silence is striking; despite the fact that it is approaching lunchtime, it is incredibly quiet. Even the few passing vehicles do not manage to disturb the tranquillity of the countryside. Joakim smiles to himself; in a very concrete way, both he and the rest of the group have embraced the calm and the silence. Even the most talkative become silent, which is not a common occurrence ...

After the walk, everyone catches their breath in the common living room. The conversation soon turns to the evening's events. Clothes and ideas are discussed and compared amid laughter. After a while, the guys break away to enjoy a beer in the sun. A guy from the neighbouring house greets Klas and invites him over. When he returns, he has a cryptic smile on his lips.

"That was Martin; I've known him for a while. He mentioned that he needed help with something for his partner before the party starts. We don't have much to do before we get ready for dinner, right?"

"Nah, I don't think so. What did he need help with?" Bengt asks curiously.

"He wanted to know if I knew any reliable guys who could give Anette, his partner, a memorable afternoon. They are both very into BDSM, and Anette is submissive. I took the liberty of saying that I absolutely had the right guys for the job. What you say?"

No further contemplation was needed; everyone wholeheartedly agreed that Anette should have a nice afternoon. After discussing their plans with their respective partners, they meet Martin at the basement entrance of the main building. Immediately they notice that even the basement level is in a sad state. It looks more like a medieval dungeon than something built in the early 20th century. An inspection tour of the dimly lit rooms only strengthens and confirms the first impression. Furniture and other furnishings were mostly missing; the only things in the gloomy rooms were a couple of aging iron beds and some spectacular BDSM items. Definitely not a place where anyone in their right mind would want to spend a night.

Martin begins by introducing Erik, a friend who joins as reinforcement. He continues with a brief review of what the arrangement looks like and emphasizes emphatically that he, and no one else, is in control.

"And remember no disturbing chatter and absolutely no talk with Anette. Just do as you're told and she will be happy, clear as mud I suppose." He fell silent and let his eyes play over the expectant guys. "Okay, then I'll go get my darling. She's tied up at the other end with a blindfold and is probably both horny and bored by now."

Before he leaves, he takes a handful of condoms out of his pocket. "These are for use, a bit boring but unfortunately necessary."

The silence that Martin commanded has not quite subsided; the boys are happy and excited like kids at a birthday party. They talk and joke until Erik discreetly whispers, "shut up, here they come!" Everyone falls silent, remembering Martin's unmistakably clear words. Anette obediently follows Martin; the chain with which he leads her is attached to a leather collar adorned with sparkling stones that any dog would envy. Despite the blindfold, she moves freely and confidently towards the waiting group. With surprise and a hint of disappointment, they note her strict dress. With her hair neatly styled and a pleated checkered skirt matched with a white blouse and black patent pumps, she resembles a strictly dressed secretary. But there is still a crucial difference; the minimal length of the skirt reveals that it is not an ordinary day at the office that awaits …

When he reaches the boys, Martin pulls lightly on the chain and Anette obediently stops to wait for the next command. He lets his gaze wander from person to person, seemingly enjoying watching both Anette and the guy's struggle with their restrained expectations. To his dismay, the boys don't quite take the moment seriously; he sighs heavily and gives the helpers an unmistakable look. The guys immediately calm down and stare at Anette in complete silence. Satisfied with the results of the silent reprimand, he unbuttons a few buttons on Anette's blouse and sternly orders her to her knees.

With a quick "Yes, master," she immediately obeys the order.

The guys wait with growing impatience for a signal, a sign from Martin that the game can begin, but nothing happens. Evidently, he enjoys seeing their impatient anticipation, deliberately waiting for the signal that everyone is waiting for.

Finally, he makes an unequivocal gesture and says the magic words. "It's time to give the bitch what she craves."

In a fraction of a second, six eager dicks appear and judging by their condition, it wasn't just Anette who was happy about those words.

Erik, Martin's friend, is the first to step forward. He grabs Anette by the hair and lets his stiff member slowly caress her lips. A brief smile appears on her lips but she remains passive…but suddenly temptation takes over, she greedily closes her lips around the treat. Martin reacts quickly, the initiative is immediately punished with a jerk in the chain and a stern call not to take your own initiative. She quickly blurts out an excuse, bows her neck and quietly waits for the next order. Erik steps aside and Klas quickly takes his seat and repeats the procedure. As the seconds tick by, Anette's breathing quickens, but this time she doesn't take any initiative of her own.

Martin shows his authority; slowly he lets the clock tick before giving her another command. An order that can hardly be misunderstood, "suck cock, you horny slut!"

Anette is quick to obey the command, and the pleasure is evidently mutual; both groan and moan with satisfaction. After Klas has had his share of Anette's attention, he steps back to make room for the next man who willingly offers his hard baton. Anette takes her task seriously and diligently works according to Martin's instructions, but the guys are eager. With her lips occupied, she does her best to satisfy the others in the line of eagerly waiting men with her hands, but it's not going so well... Apparently, women also have limitations in their multitasking ability.

Suddenly and arbitrarily, Martin interrupts the whole thing. Without a word, he grabs the chain and signals with a jerk that Anette should get up. As soon as she is on her feet, he leads her to the next room. Commands to the guys are unnecessary; they follow along curiously, what is waiting for Anette?

It is a sparsely furnished room; the only pieces of furniture are a St. Andrew's cross and something that looks like a medieval instrument of punishment. Martin leads Anette to the latter and lifts the upper part and places her hands and neck in the openings of the log. With her head and hands in place, Anette now stands with her bottom in a provocative position, left to Martin's whims. After checking the blindfold, he takes a step aside and stares at his beloved with a contented expression. He picks up a riding whip, kisses Anette's ivory white butt and tenderly asks: "Darling, have you been a naughty girl, tasted a dick or so?"

The answer comes quickly, "Yes, Master, I have been naughty, naughty and disobedient. Please punish me!"

Calmly and absently, he replies, "Well, first you have to confess your sins, you little slut."

The words flow out, "I have sucked cock, several cocks. I liked it, not just liked it, I really loved it. It was wonderful to take one by one, there must have been five or six nice hard cocks."

"Hmm, that's serious, do you have more to confess?"

"Yes, I wished everyone had squirted, filled me with cum!"

"I'm not surprised, how do you want to be punished?"

"Spank me hard, I deserve it."

"Okay, I hear what you're saying," Martin murmurs as he absentmindedly fingers Anette's wet slot. Suddenly, without warning, her protruding butt receives three heavy blows.

"Is it enough?"

Anette winces and moans, "More, much more. Whip the horniness out of my body."

"Yeah, you really are a slut. You get fifteen more, and you keep the count. And remember, it should be loud and clear!"

The guys quietly take in the spectacular role play. Some masturbate with their gaze fixed on Anette's bare ass. For a moment, time seems to stand still, but they are soon brought back to reality by Martin's authoritative voice.

"I don't want any disturbance until I say so. Right now, you can just watch and jerk off, is that understood?"

Joakim and his friends nod in agreement and watch with eager curiosity as Martin alternates between caressing and spanking Anette's bare ass. She obediently counts the strokes as her buttocks change colour from white to pink to finally take on a dark red hue. By the time she reaches eleven, the pain becomes significant, she can no longer stand still. Like a restless racehorse she stamps her feet on the floor and, in a strained voice, counts the remaining strokes.

"How are you baby? Is that enough or do you need more?" Martin asks in a surprisingly gentle voice.

"Um," hesitates Anette.

"I'll take that as a yes, I will let you try a new toy."

Martin takes out what looks like a small tennis racket, an electric bug zapper. He playfully hits Anette with it and waits for her reaction. She replies in a surprised voice, "What was that? It barely felt anything, maybe a little harder."

"Sure," Martin says with a smile and presses the device against Anette's buttocks, a spark ignites in the darkness. Her reaction is immediate; she screams and stamps her feet once again.

"What the hell did you do! It felt like you stabbed me with something sharp?"

Martin hastily explains what it was and continues without waiting for a response, but traditional spanking suits Anette better. After a few more sparks on her moist buttocks, she screams, "RED, FOR FUCK'S SAKE, RED!!"

The safe word makes Martin freeze in his movement. Without hesitation, he sticks to the agreement and abruptly ends the electrical play. He releases Anette and turns to the guys. "Well, gentlemen, what do you say, does she need spanking or cock?"

A unanimous "cock" echoes in the room, followed by a shy "Yes, please."

Martin nods and takes hold of the chain again. Despite Anette previously pulling the emergency brake, he maintains a firm grip on the reins as he guides them towards the next room. Anette obediently follows, making no serious attempt to hide her eager smile. This room, too, is sparsely furnished. The only piece of furniture is an old iron bed strategically placed in the middle of the dimly lit space. The bare, dusty light bulb above the bed fights an uneven battle against the darkness but provides enough light to carry out the third and final act. Martin leads Anette to the bed, and the guys receive one last instruction. – Give her cock, plenty of cock.

One for all, all for one, brotherly, Joakim and the other guys share the honourable task. Martin watches with satisfaction as the guys enthusiastically penetrate Anette, who clearly shows her appreciation. However, the fun comes to an abrupt end when Martin suddenly interrupts everything.

Anette tears off her blindfold and exclaims angrily, "What the hell, why did you stop it? This time you didn't hear any stop word."

Martin shrugged. "Sorry, I just thought you had enough."

With a disappointed sigh, she sits on the edge of the bed, blinks and rubs her eyes as if she has just woken up from a dream. However, the traces of the past half hour remain, confirming that it was not just a dream. Ribbons and hair are no longer neatly arranged, and the lipstick is smudged more on her cheeks than in its original place. The most eye-catching, however, are her buttocks, which transition to increasingly darker shades of red and blue. Despite the seemingly rough treatment she endured, she still smiles contentedly as she thanks the guys for their contribution. In turn, the guys express their gratitude for a delightful, decadent experience, which Klas spices up a little extra. On the spot, he offers his services to them in the future and immediately receives murmurs of agreement from the other guys.

The five musketeers return to their loved ones, who have already made significant progress in preparations for the evening. Plans are made and discussed, and tables and chairs are covered with wide dresses, wigs and makeup. All activity ceases when the guys enter the room, immediately they meet by a unanimous question - How was it, what did you do? Still tense and playful, the boys recount the events in the basement, but the picture they convey is obviously not complete. Curious and intrusive questions are asked, some answered in detail, others vaguely and briefly. None of the girls seem to mind the guy's afternoon but a twinge of envy can shine through – Five guys for one girl ... Don't forget, we need to get ours.

The masquerade and tonight's dinner are approaching relentlessly, and the guys are also forced to take on their transformation for the evening. Although their attire and makeup are simpler than the girls', the 18th-century fashion for gentlemen is not entirely uncomplicated either. After some help with powder and makeup, the guys are ready, all that remains is to capture the result of their efforts. Serious pictures are mixed with photos definitely not suitable for the family album. In a gathered group, the colorful company sets off towards the grand house and the banquet hall. Clothes and colors stand in stark contrast to the usual dress code of leather and latex, wide dresses and frock coats flapping in the evening breeze. The white, powdered faces adorned with the occasional beauty spot shine brightly in the setting sun. The atmosphere is lively, everyone expects a pleasant and eventful evening.

Aperitifs and mingling continue in a cheerful atmosphere. Most guests have successfully embraced the theme of the party, and the lively and extravagant company is truly a feast for the eyes. Susanne and Joakim share a table and their friends, and soon they share more than just the table. Dinner conversation fights an uneven battle against the goodies generously offered by both the ladies and gentlemen. The conversation goes on even when someone slides under the table to explore what's hiding under the loose dresses and knee-length pants. The wigs disappear more often under the edge of the table and the ladies' necklines get deeper and deeper. The protracted dinner puts the partygoers to the test and it only gets worse when dessert is delayed ...

When the dessert finally arrives, it is undoubtedly clear that the wait was worth it. The naked woman on the serving trolley is carefully decorated with cream and berries. Starting from her feet, the cream meanders in intricate patterns up to her stomach, where the berries gather. Her private parts are well covered with a thick layer of cream... With shameless glee, the dessert-hungry guests dig into the exclusive dessert. Unsurprisingly, the cream seems to be the favourite. It's a lovely and playful atmosphere, laughter and happy comments follow each other. Table manners oscillate between extremes, some guests are very orderly, use utensils and neatly place small portions on their plates. But most people don't care, they simply eat directly with their hands and face.

In just a few minutes the woman is literally stripped to the skin and the last sticky residue is gently licked off before she is finally rolled out for a much-needed shower.

However, the dessert has left a clear mark, many faces glisten with cream. Most of the gentlemen get away with a simple hand and face wash, but, some of the ladies have it much harder. Especially those who didn't think they needed a spoon and now have to put a lot of effort into restoring their party makeup.

The activities in the main hall have already started when Susanne and Joakim's group enter. The few sofas and armchairs are already filled with happy and horny women and men. It is not easy to find a place to settle down, even the swing in the middle of the hall is occupied. The chilly hall doesn't make it any easier to get in the mood, but eventually a sofa becomes available. Susanne and Joakim are soon up and running and working diligently to generate heat.

Suddenly they are interrupted by an enthusiastic Suddenly they are interrupted by an enthusiastic "Listen up, I have a nice surprise!"

The man continues to vaguely explain the next item on the agenda. However, there is no cheering and the mood drops a few degrees further in the already chilly ballroom. The activity begins and an awkward silence descends over the entire event. Resigned sighs and comments are heard here and there, and Kajsa suggests that they instead continue the party at home. All said and done, the seven couples from the table, along with some other party-goers, march out of the party hall to organize a party of their own.

The word spreads quickly and soon the small house is filled to the brim. Soon twenty people, maybe more than that are involved in various sexual activities. But the influx of people puts the furniture to tough tests. The beds, the sofa and even the fragile chairs are called into action in the name of passion. Kajsa and Henrik fuck on the old creaky sofa, which protests loudly. Their rhythmic thrusts make the whole sofa wobble dangerously, soon one end is well on its way to coming loose. The sofa is eventually saved by Joakim, determined to hold the fragile piece of furniture together until Kajsa and Henrik finish their fuck.

Suddenly, there's a crash. Karin and Klas, who had to settle for one of the wooden chairs, are on the floor, writhing with laughter. The chair they were just having sex on lies in pieces around them, but fortunately, no one except the chair is harmed. The poor furniture gives rise to jokes and cheerful comments about the lack of quality. Someone suggests that IKEA and other furniture manufacturers should hire the group as quality testers.

Eventually the crowd thins out, and even the occupants of the house begin to withdraw. Susanne says goodnight while Joakim lingers and finishes with some wine and small talk until the last guests have left the house. He sneaks quietly into the room, undresses in the dark and crawls down next to Susanne. He runs his hand along her body and realizes with some confusion that there are actually two women in the bed.

At Joakim's surprised exclamation, the bedside lamp lights up. Susanne is joined by Marianne, both women having a good laugh at Joakim's surprised expression when he realizes that Susanne was obviously not as tired as she claimed. The sight of the naked women arouses his desire again and Joakim is delighted at the opportunity to play with two sensual women. But the joy doesn't last long, before he even lies down Marianne yawns, hugs Susanne and thanks for a nice time. But he is not too displeased, Susanne willingly spreads her legs, but to his disappointment he is forced to realize that the mind does not always control all parts of the body. The late hour and the wine have finally taken their toll, he has no choice but to turn off the light and wait for new strength.

Childishly Fun Party

Autumn slowly turns into winter, but fortunately is the winter darkness is lightened by hot meetings and club visits and of course winter doesn't last forever... The long-awaited spring is approaching and to their delight they can soon tick off another item on their bucket list. At the beginning of May, Marianne and Bengt host an oil party in the spirit of erotica.

Eventually, lovely May arrived, and they set off for the eagerly anticipated oil party. During the car ride, the topics of conversation vary, but their upcoming vacation is the one they often return to. Susanne can't help but smile as she reminisces about the previous years in the naturist paradise. "I'm really looking forward to the oil party, but I'm even more excited for Cap d'Agde."

"Same here, but I can tell from your expression that you're thinking about sex, you horny thing. Something from Cap, perhaps?" Joakim wonders with a curious tone.

Susanne nods with a content smile. "I was thinking of the French police officer who was there on vacation. I'll never forget the day on the beach when Pernilla had the police on one side and Krister on the other. Do you remember her smile? She looked so damn satisfied while she jerking off both guys at the same time, it almost looked like she was skiing. If I remember correctly, she even fell asleep with her hands still around their dicks."

"Of course, I remember, but what was his name?" asks Joakim with a thoughtful look.

"Wasn't it Yannick or something like that?"

"Yes, that sounds familiar. He really liked being with us Swedes, but at the same time he was so worried about being recognized by his colleagues."

"Yes, there was a lot going on at the beach that year. Do you remember the Danish group that was next to us?"

"You don't forget those crazies easily," Susanne replies with an infectious laugh and continues, "I can tell by your smile that you're thinking about the champagne trick… or could it possibly be the ice dildo contest?"

"I was thinking about the champagne trick," Joakim replies, joining Susanne's happy laugh as he tries remembers the spectacular event. How was it, yes, two of the guys were holding up the blonde girl. Then her friend shook the sparkling wine, popped the cork and quickly stuffed the bottle into her pussy. My God, it was like a real fountain orgasm. I would have loved to be there and…"

Before he can continue, he is brought back to reality by Susanne's voice saying "Joakim, stop daydreaming and focus on the traffic!"

"Sure, I was just lingering on the details, it was really great. Maybe we should try to have some champagne fun when we get to Cap?"

"Yeah, it was a fun thing, but I'm not interested myself. You can ask our friends if anyone is up for it."

"I can ask them, and maybe you too ... if I bring it up at the right time," Joakim replies with a hint of disappointment in his voice.

Susanne quickly changes the topic of conversation. "Thank God, we must be close now."

"Yes, just a few kilometres left, but we're a little late. They might even have started already."

Shortly after, they turn into the driveway, and as soon as they open the car door, their question is answered – the party has begun. However, it's not moans or sounds of pleasure that can be heard. The massive cacophony of laughter and joyful shouts sounds more like a bunch of happy kindergarten children than a sex party. They knock on the door but have to wait a while before Bengt finally opens it. Naked, glistening with oil, and wearing an equally happy and silly smile, he welcomes them.

"We were a little worried when you didn't come, but we started anyway."

"We noticed it, we could hear it as soon as we got out of the car," replies Joakim and laughs heartily. "But Bengt, you don't have to worry about the neighbours. No one understands what you're up to. It sounds more like a rowdy children's party. Have you been smoking something or is it just crazy fun?"

"No one's smoking that kind of things, but I can assure you it's ridiculous fun. Hurry up and take off your clothes. And Susanne, there's absolutely no point in putting on a perfect make-up. It'll disappear in no time in the oil."

The welcome drink will have to wait while they go straight down to the cellar. Bengt happily tells how he solved the practical details. The simple but ingenious solution involved inflatable mattresses and a roll of construction plastic. By all accounts, the solution works great. The sight that greets them brings Joakim's thoughts to Dante's Inferno and his experiences in hell, but the comparison ends there. No one seems to be suffering in hellish torment. On the contrary, everyone wriggling around on the slippery surface looks ecstatically happy...

Susanne and Joakim soon become part of the euphoric mass of glistening, oil-soaked bodies. It's impossible not to get caught up in the cacophony of cheerful laughter, but the minimal friction also creates problems. Joakim quickly realizes that it is much easier to catch a slippery bar of soap than an oiled sex partner. Any attempt to transition from caressing to penetration immediately results in them drifting apart. After several futile attempts, Susanne finally comes to the rescue. She pushes Joakim and the woman against the wall and lo and behold, with Susanne's help, it finally works.

After Susanne saved Joakim, she becomes the recipient of Bengt's care. Lying on her back, she receives a thorough oil massage. She is completely covered in olive oil, and soon Bengt attempts the same feat that Joakim failed at just a moment ago, but he too has to give up. However, giving up is not an option. They try again, this time with Susanne on top, but with the same frustrating results. Joakim eventually notices their predicament and takes the opportunity to repay Susanne's kindness. With a little help, she manages to stay in position, at least for a while. Everyone seems to have similar problems, curses and laughter are heard from all sides as the relentless soap effect hits.

There is no rationing of oil, as soon as the oil runs out, Bengt refills with fresh olive oil and the guests are more than happy to help. Joakim laughs with pleasure and empties the contents of the bottle over the woman in front of him who provocatively sticks out her ass. Enchanted, he follows the path of the oil as it trickles down her buttocks, slowly turning the two halves into glistening spheres. A stream of oil collects between the buttocks and continues its journey through the glistening labia before finally falling to the ground like a sparkling waterfall. Joakim is hopelessly lost; he feels dizzy and drunk, but not from alcohol. The feeling of happiness comes from the complete feeling of sexual freedom. He lets his hands slide over his lower back towards the pleasure in front of him, the only thing in his field of vision right now. For a brief moment, he lets his hands pause before gently sliding his middle finger into her inviting anus, which accepts the intrusion without resistance. That's great, but where the hell do I find a condom?

He searches with his eyes but is soon interrupted by a voice saying, "Shit the condom, just fuck me!"

The condom suddenly feels less important and, with his finger still in the tight hole, he lets the oil-soaked, pink groove swallow his equally fat erection. The atmosphere and vision below him make it increasingly difficult to hold back ...but the problem is solved faster than he really wants. After a few more bumps, the slippery surface plays a cruel trick, sending both of them tumbling helplessly. They laugh hysterically and slide apart, and the spell is suddenly broken. Both realize the impossibility of continuing. The pleasurable intimacy they had just started had to be postponed. Eventually Bengt's oil supply runs out and one by one they head off for a much-needed shower.

But the party isn't over. Refreshed and unusually smooth-skinned, they continue their playful activities, though without oil. Susanne lends a helping hand to Yvonne as she does her best to provide Marianne with a cozy moment. Joakim is not left out either. Karola lies on her back on a small work table, spreading her legs invitingly in the air. Joakim jumps agilely onto the table and squats down, not unlike a frog ... He grabs Karola by the shoulders and fucks her with rhythmic thrusts until his leg muscles no longer want to cooperate.

Olle, who has been standing on the sidelines enjoying the show, compliments them on their acrobatic lovemaking. Joakim replies,

"It wouldn't have worked without this sturdy table."

Olle just grins and simply says, "Kinnarps quality furniture ..."

That's the final straw, and both Karola and Joakim collapse in laughter, ending yet another sexual encounter prematurely with bubbling laughter... The party continues until everyone feels satisfied or simply exhausted from oil play and sex. The activities gradually transition to casual touching and pleasant conversations, washed down with one final glass of wine before they crawl into bed.

The day after, during breakfast Bengt tells us that he is very satisfied with the oil party, the solution with air mattresses and construction plastic worked better than expected. He goes on to say that the floor did well, but then bursts into laughter.

"But the oil has left its clear marks on the walls. You have to come down and see for yourself, there are oily handprints, footprints and butt marks everywhere. It looks rather suspicious to say the least, the only option is to repaint the walls. It will be my Sunday project, and Kalle has promised to help."

Back home, they realize that vacation is still a distant dream, but they focus on the saying that planning is half the fun. They have already booked the ferry and the apartment, so all that remains is to decide the route and daily stops. The trip goes through the Netherlands and includes a stop at a club. It sparks a lively debate: Should they bet on a safe card like Fun4Two or try another well-known Dutch club, perhaps Fata Morgana?

Unforgettable parties and moments

A few weeks later, Susanne is sitting and scrolling on her mobile phone "Joakim, come here, immediately!"

"Did we hit the jackpot or what?"

Susanne laughs happily and points to the email. "We haven't won anything, but this isn't bad either. We've been invited to a wedding… a swingers wedding!"

"How nice, but I didn't know we had any friends who were thinking of getting married."

"No, me neither. It's Leonie and Eddo, and it fits almost perfectly into our planning for the trip home from Cap. Admittedly, we have to leave the apartment a day early and we won't make it to any clubs on the way home, but we'll have to put up with that."

Joakim smiles happily, "It's okay with me, we can't miss a wedding like that. Do they write where it is?"

"They live in Breda, so both the wedding and the party will probably be there somewhere. They would come back a little later with more info."

Eventually July comes to an end and with the car packed to the brim, they head south towards Trelleborg and the ferry to Sassnitz. After two stops at bed and breakfasts, they finally pass the last roundabouts in Cap. The now familiar procedure for new arrivals no longer feels so complicated, even if waiting in the overcrowded reception area tests patience. So close ... but not quite there yet. They have to wait a little longer before they can finally exchange their travel clothes for their birthday suits. Walking freely as you were created has become something natural and self-evident, something that doesn't have anything to do with sex. Here, the often-elusive equality feels closer than ever. Under the banner of naturism, the usual divisions of gender, social groups and so on fades away.

Kajsa and Henrik have already been there for a few days and can share highly interesting party news.

"Susanne, did you hear when Henrik talked about the Dutch party on Tuesday? It sounded really exciting. He'll check if it's okay to invite another couple, and with some luck, we might receive an invitation during the evening."

"Oh yes, I heard. Kajsa told me a bit about last year's party. There were fifteen or sixteen couples, mostly Dutch but also some German and French couples. Additionally, they had arranged three single guys who served champagne and fulfilled any wishes the ladies had. Kajsa thought the whole event was very successful, like a mingle party spiced up with sex."

A couple of hours later, they receive a text message. They quickly skim through the few lines. No discussion is needed, this party is not something they can't miss. The writing is extremely clear and appealing:

You are most welcome to a spectacular midnight orgy in the dunes of Cap. Please respect the following simple but important rules:

- *Confirm participation by Monday, as latest.*
- *Bring a bottle of champagne (entrance fee).*
- *Dress code women: Sexy slut, high heels.*
- *Dress code men: pimp style.*
- *Party starts at midnight, please respect time.*
- *Use a flashlight for the walk in the dunes.*
- *Bring your own condoms.*

After we receive your confirmation, on the same evening as the party, we will send you information on where to find the hotspot.

Horny regards, Hannah & Eddie

The confirmation is sent without delay. Despite a pleasant day at the beach in the company of Kajsa and Henrik, they can't help but impatiently look forward to the evening. The four leave a little earlier than usual to have time to rest before the evening's adventure. Eagerly, they await the text that will guide them to the party somewhere among Cap's dunes. After a long wait, the phone finally comes to life.

Joakim sighs annoyed. "Why are they making us wait so long?"

Susanne nods in agreement. "Shit, what are they saying?"

Joakim reads quickly the few lines. "Start from the beach restaurant at midnight. Behind the lifeguard cabin is a path marked with solar cell lights."

"How long does it take from here?"

"Well…fifteen minutes should be enough if you take something comfortable to walk in."

"Absolutely, I'll take the fuck boots in a bag."

Just before midnight, they arrive at the sleeping beach restaurant. Despite the darkness, they see several couples sneaking among the dunes, clearly with the same goal as themselves. They join the silhouettes stumbling along the solar-powered lights. At first only the sound of the sea is heard, but after only a couple of minutes the rhythmic songs of the waves are mixed with the hum of happy voices. After a few more turns among the dunes, a lighted area with high tent walls appears. At the entrance they are met by a well-built man in his mid-thirties, wearing only tight underwear and a matching bow tie. He politely greets the arriving couples, checks the names against the guest list and collects the entrance fee; the champagne and places it in a cooler with other bottles.

The Dutch have really made an effort. In just a few hours, they have created a comfortable oasis in the middle of the dunes with simple means. Almost half of the surface inside the tent walls is covered with thick inflatable mattresses in various shapes and sizes. The area is lit by an oil lamp and about ten helium-filled condoms with small LED lights enclosed. The condom lamps, slowly swaying in the faint night breeze, cast a soft enchanting glow that further enhances the slightly surreal atmosphere.

But it's not just the practical arrangements that surprise them; the whole event in the middle of the dunes feels improbable. Not least the sight of all the dressed-up women and men who have clearly put a lot of effort into following the prescribed dress code; sluty style for women and pimp-inspired attire for men. The feeling is also enhanced by the presence of the elegant Chippendale impersonators who except the champagne offer all kind of services. After everyone introduce themselves, the merry mingling continues, but it doesn't last very long. Several guests are more than eager and barely drink their first glass of champagne before occupying the mattresses. After fifteen, maybe twenty minutes, the majority, including Susanne and Joakim, leave the social activities behind.

Even the hostess joins the game, temporarily forgetting her duties and succumbing to the temptation to try some sweets. Standing on all fours, she satisfies the man on the mattress in front of her. Bare-breasted and

wearing a black leather corset, she is an irresistible delight
to the eyes. Although she is sexier than sluty, she makes
up for this deviation from the dress code with her actions. Her entire presence, especially her nicely shaped
ass, commands attention and Joakim wastes no time in
responding to the call. God what a butt, best to make a
move before someone else does. He begins with gentle
caresses of her buttocks and immediately receives an appreciative look. Without wasting any time, he takes the
opportunity to make a good impression on the hostess
and at the same time get a chance to enjoy her inviting
body.

Susanne is not idle either; she tries out the mattresses
together with one of the eager Chippendale impersonators. Granted, he is considerably younger than her usual
prey, but who asks about age in the heat of the moment?
Afterwards, she stays on the mattress, enjoying the moment and waiting for Joakim.

"I saw you were having fun with one of the younger
fellows," said Joakim with a smile.

"Oh yeah," replies Susanne and carry on with a happy
face. "He wasn't that old, but he actually took the initiative. We talked and he started caressing me, here and
there. I got so fucking horny, hadn't he insisted on having
sex, I probably would have forced myself on him.

"Age doesn't matter in this context, but otherwise we don't choose boys or girls his age."

Susanne nodded. "We haven't, but he was charming and surprisingly experienced for his age. By the way… I saw you had a good time with Hannah; at least it looked like you did?"

Joakim smiles. "Absolutely, I was completely mesmerized by her delicious ass when she gave head to the French guy."

"She has a great ass; I would have loved to be there and help. But now I think we'll take a break... Have a glass of bubbly and talk to Kajsa and Henrik, if they're not busy?"

"Looks like they're going to take a break too."

Susanne gives Henrik a big hug. "Henrik, you bloody Duracell rabbit, how can you stand it?"

But before Henrik can answer, Kajsa says cheerfully. "For once, it's actually me who has been more diligent than Henrik ..."

After refuelling and socializing, they return to the lively orgy pit with renewed energy. Things quickly escalate, without even knowing who took the initiative, they are right in the middle of a fun and pleasurable sex act with a Dutch couple. They get yet another confirmation that the Dutch are an open-minded bunch and Susanne and Joakim in turn do their best to live up to the prevailing image of Swedes as sexually liberated.

Eventually, the dropping temperature and the raw, damp sea breeze make their presence felt. The crowd of partygoers slowly shrinks and eventually Susanne and Joakim also say goodbye to the Dutch couples who arranged it. Now the darkness was even denser than before and the solar-powered lights that show the way have gone out. The flashlight they were advised of now comes in handy. Satisfied and happy to have gotten to know some of the Dutch couples, they leave the sex oasis behind. However, they only get intimate with a few of the couples, but quality comes before quantity…

The carefree days are slowly coming to an end, but this time the departure feels easier than usual. The wedding in Holland, just two days away, keeps spirits up. They set their GPS for Breda and are finally able to park their car at the Golden Tulip Hotel.

The next day, the wedding bells ring for Leonie and Eddo. The informal part of the wedding is held on a small farm, just a stone's throw from Breda's largest canal, the Marken. The picturesque farm, owned by Leonie and Eddo's best friends, guarantees an undisturbed evening. In the Dutch way, the wedding is divided into two parts. First the obligatory civil ceremony in the town hall, followed by an informal evening ceremony usually conducted by a priest according to old traditions. However, Leonie and Eddo's swinger friends have the privilege of skipping the bureaucratic civil ceremony in Breda's old town hall. Now all that remains is the wedding reception, where a relaxed and romantic ceremony awaits.

Not surprisingly, they will be married by a close friend who is a priest in the Protestant church and, of course, also a swinger. After a happy and lively mingling, the guests gather for the wedding ceremony. Both the bride and groom and the guests are dressed for the festive occasion, but without the classic wedding clothes. Leather and latex dominate, but perhaps with slightly lighter colors than usual.

The groom wears a regular coat, but that's where the tradition ends. The formal shirt has been replaced by a t-shirt with latex details, and the dress pants have been replaced by a pair of latex shorts. The bride's outfit also does not resemble the traditional bridal attire. The minimal dress, although it is white, is completely different from the usual one. The thigh-high boots barely reach up to what can hardly be called a dress. Surprisingly, she wears a pair of minimal thongs as well as a bra that doesn't hide her bust, rather accentuates it and exposes her breasts in a delicate way.

Appreciative comments pour in on the bride and groom, and to everyone's delight, even the priest is quick to agree with the praise for the choice of wedding attire. The ceremonial dialogue during the wedding ceremony is in Dutch but the little that Susanne and Joakim understand still paints the picture of a very traditional and proper wedding. The previously happy atmosphere has subsided and both the bride and groom and the guests are absorbed in the seriousness of the moment. Apart from the chanting of the priest, the only sounds are somewhat muffled sniffing and rustling of handkerchiefs. After the ceremony is over and the groom kisses the bride as usual, all traditions end. Amid general rejoicing, the bride receives an extremely intimate embrace and a long, deep kiss from the zealous priest.

After all, the dinner reception has some traditional elements, which are, however, lightened up with crazy antics, both at and around the table. Several guests also take the opportunity to congratulate the couple with primarily physical and tangible gifts. Although both Susanne and Joakim are used to these situations, towards the end of the evening they witness something that makes them raise their eyebrows. The ultimate wedding gift is given by the good priest. At a mutual request from the new married couple, the spiritual advisor, now dressed in a leather suit, pays his tribute to the bride in an entirely different kind of act. Leaning over a table, Leonie receives the priest's salvation in a very concrete way ...

The end of the holiday could not have been better. At home in Sweden, they feel satisfied and full of energy to face upcoming challenges, both in their everyday life and in the swinger world. This time they also have a whole new challenge to contend with. Both agree that their experiences since opening up their sex life must be written down. It will be a tribute to the swinger lifestyle and, above all, a declaration of love to all the wonderful people they have met since they set out on their journey on the sea of free sexuality.

Epilogue

Since we entrusted the mission of reliving our memories to our alter egos: Susanne and Joakim, what could be better than letting them finish the story? If they were flesh and blood, they would probably have a lot of thoughts, maybe it would have sounded like this ...

"Joakim, I feel incredibly grateful that we had the opportunity to relive everything they experienced"

"Me too, clearly they've had an interesting and eventful sex life. Despite some hiccups, most of it has been positive. I can only agree and say that it's been an equally fun and delightful journey. But it's not just about sex , think of all their wonderful friends they had the privilege of getting to know."

Susanne replies thoughtfully, "Their closest friends in the swinger world obviously mean a lot to them, but what would it be like without sex? Isn't sex a kind of glue that holds them together?"

"Sex is certainly one of the cornerstones, but I think their closest swinger friends mean more than that?"

"But Joakim, sex is important in all relationships, whether it's a couple relationship or in this case, the relationship between couples? For it to work in the long run, everyone involved needs to be horny, happy and grateful, or in other words ... be curious and have the ability to appreciate and make the most of our short time on mother earth."

Joakim replies with a thoughtful expression. "Oh, that sounded a bit philosophical, but I totally agree with you. But I guess it's not just about their closest friends, they've also met a lot of fun and interesting people just for one night. Also, the quirky characters they worried at the beginning seems to have been more or less absent It may also be that they simply have not felt the need to explore the more extreme expressions that exist on the fringes of their world.

"No, they haven't taken to the really weird inclinations, but they've definitely taken some wild and crazy turns. But you know, I've been thinking about something else," Susanne continues. "Is it all really true? Much of what they experienced is only imagination for most, if even that."

"Hmm, good question ... They claim that everything they relate to is recreated to the best of their ability, but there is a catch. In the preface they mention that certain episodes are depicted from the perspective of an observer."

"Are we really supposed to believe that?" Susanne answered with a skeptical tone.

"Well, personally, I think they've been more or less involved in most of the events, and probably even more."

"Sure, but it would be interesting to know what they were just spectators to. They can't have missed much, for my part I would have liked to stay a little longer in their world, don't you feel the same way?"

"Absolutely, I would have liked to have stayed on for a few more chapters. It feels sad to step off, rest, or however you want to put it," replied Joakim with a touch of melancholy in his voice.

"Will there be a sequel, a part two? Maybe, when they've checked off more items on their bucket list?"

"Who knows? In any case, I can't imagine them stopping the swinger life just because they're getting older. As long as they're healthy and not too fragile, they'll probably take their swinger habits into the retirement world. There's no chance they'll stop," Susanne agrees. with a nostalgic look.

Joakim is caught by Susanne's mood. "I really hope there's a sequel, and like you said, if not sooner, maybe we'll get a chance to relive this after they've passed the retirement line. It would be really nice to reconnect with their cozy, horny friends. I'm willing to bet there's a lot going on at senior retreats and similar gatherings."

"Definitely," replies Susanne and continues. "The claim that the body's pleasure value decreases as you age is probably greatly exaggerated. Retired people have plenty of time, they can't just babysit grandchildren and attend politically correct senior meetings ..."

***